Larry the Horrible Time Traveler

Larry the Horrible Time Traveler, Volume 1

Andrew Coltrin

Published by Partly Robot Industries, 2021.

LARRY THE HORRIBLE TIME TRAVELER

©2014 Andrew Coltrin

Second Edition Published July 2021

ISBN 978-1-7375049-1-7

Partly Robot Industries

P.O. Box 220121

Milwaukie, OR 97269

www.partlyrobot.com

Dedicated to all the robots.

And to all the dinosaurs.

Time Travelers often keep detailed diaries of their adventures. They do it, as much as anything else, as a way to keep track of their own timelines, and, perhaps, to keep from losing their minds in the face of it all. It doesn't always work. The following narrative has been largely pieced together from the diaries of two such travelers, Larry and Ishmael. Some gaps are filled in from documents found in the Cross-Time Coordinating Agency Archives. Other bits are just made up, but they're probably close to what actually happened, or will happen, or was heroically prevented from happening. Sadly, the jury is out on whether these two managed to make it out with their minds intact.

-Lizzabits Wal, witness to history and library intern at the Cross-Time Coordinating Agency Archives

Chapter 1
A Less than Stunning First Impression

I'VE MET A LOT OF OTHER time travelers in the field. There are times and places, or places and times, hell I don't know which comes first, but there are a few of them where the time travelers practically outnumber the unwitting and chronometrically fixed members of the teeming masses of the human race. As much as I can help it, I try to avoid those times and places, because, for the most part, I've got better things to do. I had just finished up doing one of them when I first ran into Larry.

There's no point in going into the details of the job I'd wrapped up. It was a down and dirty, quick and tidy little thing that paid reasonably well for my time and expertise. It also may have required the indulgence in a few of the kinds of temporal accounting indiscretions I like to make sure stay off the books. But that's not my point here. My point is, it was time for a drink and I knew of a bar near the waterfront that had some of the best scotch whiskey the Gilded Age had to offer. Like just about everything else in San Francisco, it had come in from around the Horn, a voyage that added just the right amount of nausea and desperation to the liquor's aging process.

I WAS ENJOYING IT. I really was. There's a certain level of sublime, mature, soul-fulfilling relaxation that is hard to come by in this world, and I was there.

Anyway, I was enjoying my drink when a loud, anachronistically dressed idiot wandered into the bar and burst my precious personal bliss bubble.

"Spring break!" he shouted at the bartender, "that's what I'm talkin' about, boy-yee!"

I don't like to through the word idiot around lightly, but it was obvious that Larry was a stupendously bad time traveler. I wanted to believe he was just pretending to be an idiot. He was loud, obnoxious, flagrantly visibly out of place, and very, very drunk. All things any seasoned time traveler knows, if you're going to make a trip like that, you're going to have a bad time. As much as I tried to imagine a scenario that justified it, I just couldn't. It was no pretense. Larry was an idiot.

It took him hours to realize he had wound up in the 19th Century. You would think all the meticulously groomed facial hair Age might have tipped him off. Apparently he was from one of those neighborhoods where the beardage was plausible. I doubt he was from one of those neighborhoods that lacks light switches, though. Of all the rubes, newbs, and greenhorns I had run into in the field, Larry's inexplicable obliviousness scored him the top honors.

I needed to intervene quickly and subtly before he did something that screwed up my interest in the timeline. Granted, the worst he could have done at that point is introduce the Macarena to the world a hundred years too soon. I suppose, worse than that, he might find himself killed.

It looked like he was already on that track as it was.

He had talked himself into the good graces of a steamship's press gang. They were getting him good and liquored up for the surprise of his lifetime, an all-expense paid cruise to the South Pacific and points further.

"Lawrence, my boy," said the press gang's particularly beefy foreman, "just wait till you see the girls in Tahiti."

"Dude," said Larry, "you have no idea. Last spring break I was in Ft. Lauderdale. MTV was there. Kurt Loder. Jenny McCarthy and all that *Singled Out* shit. Anyway, there were these chicks at one of the after parties who, you're never going to believe this—"

He paused dramatically and took a sip of his drink. He coughed, cleared his throat, and totally lost the thread of his story.

"What is in this? Is there something funny in this?" He coughed again.

I should have left him be. I should have just walked away. Davy Jones would have claimed him soon enough. But I took pity on him and his flannel and his 'No Fear' T-shirt. How he'd stumbled into Mark Twain's San Francisco was a dangerous mystery that, despite my more anti-authoritarian inclinations, I knew needed to be called to the attention of the Agency. But how involved did I personally need to be? Maybe an anonymous note would be enough.

It was hard to justify spending much energy on the kid when he obviously wasn't spending much energy on himself. Even his skepticism was half-assed.

He took another swig of his suspect drink before waiting for an answer from the man who bought the round.

"My special cocktail," said the foreman, his arm around Larry in the avuncular manner of confidence men and world class pickpockets. "A pint of ale, a shot of whiskey and a little secret ingredient I picked up in Chinatown."

"Oh," said Larry, "that's good. For a minute I thought you were trying to roofie me." He took another drink, then did a spit take. "Wait a minute. You are trying to roofie me, you sick bastard."

Dammit. So long as he was going to put up something a fight, I thought I might as well step in.

"Let the kid go, Cap," I said, letting show an ugly little piece of metal I keep up my sleeve for moments like this.

Not a gun.

No.

Guns can be handy, but when you're a time traveler, they don't always communicate what you want them to. Show up in the wrong century with a gun and no one will take you seriously until you start making noise with it. And then you've given someone an idea and changed the course of history. So I don't ordinarily carry one.

No, this ugly piece of metal was one of those ridiculously vicious looking knives-slash-can openers like they sell at truck stops in the middle of the Arizona desert. It might be designed for fighting, or it might be a prop for a Klingon sequence in a Star Trek movie, either way it looks like it could put a hole in someone when wielded by an unstable individual. And only an unstable individual would choose to wield such a thing. At least that's the theory.

"That's quite a harpoon you've got there, sailor," said the gang foreman.

"Aye," I said.

Damn. My ugly piece of metal looked like a harpoon point. Not outright unsettling, the way I'd hoped, but more par for the course in a sailor dive like the one we happened to be in. I quickly rifled through whatever mental notes I still had on *Moby-Dick*. Not much. All I could really remember is that those whalers were crazy fuckers, and maybe that could still play into my hand.

"Woah, guys," said Larry, the horrible time traveler. "It's cool. No need to, you know, go poking each other or anything. I know this is Frisco. I just didn't know this was *that* kind of a bar. Why don't I just settle up," he said, taking one of those crappy orange Velcro wallets out of his back pocket and waving to the barkeep. "And I'll move on to another venue, hopefully one with some college girls, if you know what I mean."

"Ah, Lawrence," said the foreman, "I'm afraid that our ship is sailing within the hour and we still have a couple vacancies in our crew."

A knowing chuckle passed like a wave through the entire saloon.

It suddenly became very clear that everyone in the bar was in some way or another affiliated with the impressment operation. Barkeep, bouncers, even the whores joined in a ring around us that promised nothing but pain.

"And we could always make use of an experienced harpooneer."

The foreman grinned in a way that showed me press gang foremen were every bit the crazy fuckers that career whalers are.

"Jesus, Cap," I said. "The least you could do is buy me a drink first."

I'd been in these kinds of situations before, and since my method of time travel was of the mechanical variety, a pocket watch, specifically, all I had to do was wait. All I needed was a quiet minute alone and, poof, I could be gone. But damned if I didn't feel responsible for Larry, and for what he might do to the timelines. I didn't know what his method of travel was, and I doubted he knew either. He could have been a Natural, I supposed, with the innate ability. But Naturals usually had the problem of not being able to bring their clothes with them. This guy looked like he'd just got kicked out of a Pearl Jam concert. So, for his sake, and the sake of the continuum, I had to keep an eye out for him. At least until I had an opportunity to be find out what he knew.

Reluctantly, I turned my weapon over to the foreman and gestured that I would follow where he led. The press gang were surprisingly gentle on us after that. Perhaps they felt a little sorry for us, knowing which ship we were bound for.

"Stick close to me," I said to Larry. "And do what I do."

"Dude," said Larry. "Are they taking us to their sex dungeon to harpoon us?"

"Maybe, but not before we're past the twelve mile limit," I said.

"Twelve miles," said Larry. "What kind of speed limit is that?"

"Right now, Larry, the less said, the better."

The gang corralled us through a back room as gingerly as men who live their lives as the honest purveyors of a brutal trade are able. A couple times Larry got a loving tap from a cudgel for breathing too loud. I didn't fare too badly, having practiced the art of projecting the air of a man who knows damn well it's in his best interest to play nice, but who also knows he can take down two or three others if things get ugly. Maybe only one or two others. It's hard to know how strong the effect of my attitude was in the darkened stairway and the low ceilinged corridors they jostled us through.

It wasn't long, though, before we were shown to the gangway of one of the ugliest steamers I'd ever seen. She desperately needed to be stripped of barnacles, repainted and, while they're at it, burned for firewood. I was surprised it could stay afloat, much less leave port. No wonder the skipper had trouble keeping her crewed.

"Welcome aboard the *SS Dogturd*," a sailor said as we made our way onto the deck.

"Seriously?"

"That's what we call her," the sailor said. "If you care to read the proper name off the bow, we'd all love to hear what it is."

"Dude," said Larry. "I've been to some divey places, but I don't know about this boat."

"Oh, she surprises all of us," said the sailor. "Don't you worry."

"I don't worry," I said. "I've seen the future."

"Have you now?" said the sailor.

"Yes," I said. "I believe it involves young Larry and I in a very hot place shoveling coal."

"... I knew it was a sex dungeon," said Larry. "I trusted you, old dude. But this is bullshit."

The sailor laughed, cackled really, until he doubled over in a brief coughing fit. Recovering himself, he patted Larry on the back and said, "that's the old *Dogturd* spirit. Right this way. That boiler's not going to get up a head of steam on her own."

At this point, Larry gave me the first hint of any spirit and initiative on his part by kicking me shin. I am usually slow to committing an actual violent act, but this had been building up.

"Listen, you accidental little shit," I said, grabbing him by his thriftscore flannel collar, lifting him up off the deck. "I'm not sure if you're aware of this, but I'm risking my own ass for you. I really don't have to. But here you are, wandering into the middle of my business, a complete and total fuck up of a grunge-head party rocker, about to bring down Lord knows what kind of damage upon yourself and everyone around you. Plus, I lost my really nasty knife thing. I loved that piece of metal. We'd seen some good times. And now it's gone because I've got your sorry and ignorant butt to look out for. So just keep your mouth shut and shovel some coal. It'll keep you alive while I figure some things out."

The sailor intervened, prying us apart with a long handled piece of nautical equipment.

"Save that energy for the engine room, lads. The Skipper will be waking up from his drunk soon. If we're not underway, he'll throw one of you into the fire."

He led us below decks through the heart of the boat to just as black and sinister a furnace room as you could imagine. Soot covered every surface and each and every air molecule. Shovels and coal scuttles littered the floor by the entry. A mound of coal lay beneath the mouth of a chute protruding from the bulkhead above. Lumps of blackness hailed intermittently from the chute, replenishing the mound for every shovelful removed by the men who were already on the job. Three burly stokers formed a processional, running shovels full of the fossil fuel directly into the opened jaws of hell.

It occurred to me that it might be quite a while before I got a chance to talk to Larry one to one. I considered bailing on him.

"Wait a minute," said Larry, suddenly connecting to the world around him. "Why are we shoveling coal? Is this like the 1800s, or something?"

I *seriously* considered bailing on him.

Chapter 2
The SS Dogturd

"YES, LARRY," I SAID. "This *is* the 1800s. You have no idea how you got here, do you?"

"That's nuts," said Larry. "Nice poker face, though."

The kid still had no idea what kind of situation he had gotten himself into. He refused to believe the information available to his senses, even as he hoisted a shovel full of coal into the mouth of the furnace on the *SS Dogturd*.

"Who set this all up?"

"You tell me, Larry," I said, leaning on my own shovel.

I wasn't about to work up any more of a sweat than I had to. We'd just gotten there, and the mate who brought us down to the engine room promptly disappeared. The other stokers seemed to be making the traditional half-assed effort of the underpaid and unsupervised, so I saw no reason to jump in too early. Larry, on the other hand, was shoveling like a fiend.

"I bet it was Vance," he said. "That dude's loaded. He'd spring for a setup like this just to watch me shit my pants. Like I'd give him the pleasure."

I stood and marveled as Larry out-shoveled the three seasoned stokers, who kept the slow pace of men who knew they'd be doing this all day, and into the night, and again the next day and the day after that, and that there was no point in hurrying. One by one they took a look at Larry, did a bit of quick mental calculation, and leaned on their own shovels.

"What's he in a rush for?" one of them asked. He was small and wiry compared to the other two. Compared to me? Let's just say I felt it in my best interest to stay on friendly terms with the guy.

"Hell if I know," I said. "I just happened to be at the same bar when he got Shanghaied. He doesn't even know what he's in for, yet."

"And how did you get caught up with him?" the comparatively wiry stoker asked.

"Couldn't keep my mouth shut," I said.

"How long do you think he'll keep going?"

"Dude, this sucks," Larry whined.

Of course he'd whine. Anyone with a soul patch and an LL Bean flannel shirt who found himself in the bowels of a 19th century steamer would whine. I wanted to whine, but I knew damn well what I was getting myself into when I decided to stick my neck out for the kid.

"Seriously, dude, what the fuck do I call you, anyway?"

"Call me Ishmael," I said.

"Right, Ishmael," he said, not even catching the Melville reference, and what did I expect? This deluded fool was still caught in the middle of MTV spring break. In Larry's time Kurt was still alive and pop culture misery was a viable commodity. Reading wouldn't be this one's strong suit. A shame because, if you're going to be a time traveler, it really doesn't hurt to crack a book every now and then.

"What the fuck are we doing on this boat?"

"We've been Shanghaied, Larry," I said.

"Well, duh," he said. "But why are we shoveling coal?"

"You're shoveling coal," said the wiry stoker, "because you're probably not worth a shit at doing anything else on this boat."

"Save cleaning head," said one of the other stokers.

"Granted," said the wiry one. "But when was the last time the head was cleaned on this boat?"

"You're right," said the second man. "They're absolutely filthy. I usually just hang me bum over the side and let her go, rather."

The third stoker, a quiet giant of a man, suddenly hurled his shovel at the bulkhead. It clanged loudly against the wall, bringing the conversation, and the flow of Larry's shoveling to a dead stop.

"I'm getting a drink," he said. Then he turned and ducked out of the hatch.

The other two quickly followed suit.

Before disappearing out the hatch, the wiry one turned and said, "keep the boiler hot for us, or we'll kill you when we get back."

"This is bullshit," Larry said.

"You act like you've never had a job before," I said. "This is actually one of my better first day experiences."

"How come you aren't shoveling?" said Larry.

"Because I know I'm not getting paid for it. Put your shovel down."

"Those dudes are totally going to kick our asses."

"Only if we're still here when they get back," I said. "I've got a method of travel, you've got a method of travel. All we have to do is—"

"What's this, then!" a shrill shout sounded from the coal chute above us.

"Team-building exercise!" I hollered back.

"If I don't see any shoveling by the time I get down there, my cat's going to taste so much of your backs you won't be troubled by hot bunkmates till we get to Honolulu."

"Larry," I said. "What's your method."

"I don't know what you're talking about," he said.

"We're about to get flogged, Larry. This is not 1993. You got here somehow. How did you do it? What's your method?"

"What the fuck are you talking about?"

"What," I said, "is your method of time travel?"

"You," said Larry, "are out of your mind."

I gave up trying to reason with him. Maybe he'd just stumbled into it. Maybe he was just fated to die on the *SS Dogturd*, or whatever the ship's real name was. He'd be another face on a milk carton back when he came from, and history would heal the hole around him.

Or he just might survive and go on to cause the kind of space-time paradox that would scramble the timeline and put me out of business.

I liked my job. I worked for myself, set my own hours, and could meet my clients wherever and whenever the best drink specials were. But it depended on the timeline remaining relatively stable. As much as I didn't want to do anything that might involve the enforcement division of the Cross-Time Coordination Agency, I couldn't afford to risk letting the kid out of my sight before I could tip them off, either.

Some situations are just lose-lose.

Or even lose-lose-lose more.

I could hear heavy, foreboding footsteps coming from a direction I felt must be aft. A heavy, foreboding voice accompanied it.

"You debutants are about to need to grow a new hide to cover your arses!"

A vicious sound split the air, not entirely unlike the sound you'd expect a whip with nine flails at the end would make.

"Larry," I said, "whatever you think is going on doesn't matter. We have to run. Now!"

"Gotcha, bra," he said as we tore off in the opposite direction of the flailing sound.

Racing through the passageways and holds of a fully loaded steamer that's just left port is not unlike having a go at one of those inflatable obstacle courses they have at carnivals and birthday party establishments, with a few notable exceptions. Those being chiefly that nothing's inflatable, all the edges tend to be hard and rigid, very hot steam pipes appear in the oddest places, and you are being chased by a large, hung-over ship's officer who wants to remove as much skin from your body as permissible by the customs of a longstanding maritime tradition of leadership through cruelty.

"This is really elaborate," Larry said as he shinnied up a large crate between us and a hatch leading to the deck, and, hopefully more maneuvering room.

"This is global capitalism in its teen years," I said.

"Just imagine doing this in a hold stacked with 80,000 cargo containers."

"There's no way Vance could pull off all of this," Larry gasped. It might have been one crate too far, but the sound of the cat-o-nine-tails cracking against a bulkhead helped push him over the top. "What the hell is going on?"

"I told you, Larry. You're a time traveler. I don't know how you did it. Apparently *you* don't know how you did it, either. I've got a pocket watch with extra dials. That's how I do it."

I held it out to show him. It was a family heirloom that had been given to me by my dying great-great grandfather on the condition that, when I'm about to face my end, I bring it back to him on his 21st birthday. I never knew if that last part was a joke, but I also never felt close enough to dying to find out. The pocket watch was a sturdy piece worthy of a railroad conductor or a junior member of Congress. It was waterproof, heat resistant, and told the time in centuries, decades, and weeks. Curiously, it also played MP3s and came pre-loaded with a very eclectic mix. Pretty much everything from J.S. Bach to Wesley Willis.

I never did get a chance to ask great-great grandpa about how the watch worked, and I never will. One of the Laws of Time is that the watch can never cross its own path. The next time I see great-great grandpa will be the first time he ever holds the watch. I guess he knows as much about it as I do. One of the greatest mysteries the universe holds for me is the question, who loaded it up with all that music?

"I guess that's cool," said Larry.

"You're used to guessing your way through life, aren't you?" I said, popping open the hatch and ducking out into the night. The shadows were deep, and there was no moon. The way we'd come was too narrow for our pursuer, so we had some time.

"All right, Larry. I have to know what's going on. Tell me everything you remember happening before you wound up in that bar."

"Right," he whispered as we crept across the deck, trying to put as much distance between us and the cat-o-nine-tails as possible. "Well, I'd been in San Diego for a few days. I was taking a little road trip. Visiting some Cali girls, if you know what I mean?"

"I guess."

"So I was at this awesome party. Kurt was on the stereo and this one chick was like, I'm hungry. And this other chick said there's an all night taco cart a few blocks away, and I was like, hey, I'll go with you. Safety in numbers, right? So me and these two smoking hot girls go to this taco truck and they've got all the usual stuff, right, but then they have this sign that says 'try the dino-fish tacos, if you dare.' So of course I dare, and they were kind of chewy, but all right. Then, all the other guys must have bailed on me-"

"Other guys?" I asked.

"I mean chicks. Totally hot chicks... All right, so I lied. I was with a couple dudes. And they dared me to try the dino-fish tacos. And then, bam, they ditched me and I couldn't figure out how to get back to the party, and then I found that bar where I met you."

"Must be some interesting tacos," I said, formulating a theory, not only as to the true gender of his late night munchy compadres, but also as to what triggered his accidental time jump.

"Yeah," he said. "A little chewy, but all right. I got another one," he said, pulling an actual taco, wrapped in grease soaked yellow paper, out of his back jeans pocket. "You want want a bite?"

"No thanks," I said. I marveled at the sheer dumb luck of his managing to survive in the world at all as he devoured his leftovers.

"Your loss, dude."

And then, without much fanfare, Larry suddenly wasn't there. The little bastard had his method in his back pocket the whole time.

I reached for my watch to get myself the hell out of there. Before I could set it, though, a hand clenched tight around my arm and a heavy, foreboding voice jaunted violently into my ears.

"Gotcha!"

Chapter 3
In the time of Chimpanzees

I HATE IT WHEN THEY say 'gotcha.' It just rubs my nose in the fact that I've been cornered by someone I really should have been able to outsmart. I know, it's a matter of personal pride of the sort that takes the chief position in any medieval parade of the Seven Deadly Sins. But, dammit, I take pride in my work, and a big part of my work involves not getting caught.

So, when the hulking gorilla of a first mate on the *SS Dogturd*, a ship that's most likely doomed to sink long before it could reach Santa Cruz, let alone Panama, or wherever the next port of call might be. I hadn't been paying too much attention to the particulars as the press gang manhandled me and Larry onto the boat. Now, Larry was gone, having popped back to whatever grunge-hole he'd come from, and I was dangling by my wrist from the first mate's clenched fist.

Forgive the excessive gratuities in bouncing from tense to tense. When you're a time traveler the particulars of when the hell you are in the context of telling your story can get a bit fuzzy in the best of circumstances.

This was far from the best of circumstances. I knew that there were some very lucrative business contacts waiting to be made, one, in particular was looking pretty good and only required me to meet a guy a few stumbles down from the waterfront bar back in Frisco. And now, thanks to Larry, I'd missed my appointment and was instead looking at the business end of the first mate's cat o' nine tails. Quite frankly, the circumstances sucked.

I'd been in the process of setting my watch, that family heirloom time travel device passed down from my great-great-grandfather to me and from me to my great-great-grandfather in a way that would challenge Stephen Daedalus' algebraic reasoning concerning Hamlet's grandson. Now, my left hand, which was holding the watch, was inconveniently far from my right, as the first mate stretched my arm above my head while my feet danced about looking for purchase on the deck below.

And I'm not a small guy, but any means. This first mate was a mountain.

"Right, lads," said the mate. "Anyone want to tell the new crewman here what happens when someone abandons their post without leave?"

A discomforting mob of socially maladjusted seamen had gathered to observe the culmination of the previous chapter's chase and my unfortunate capture.

"The cat! The cat! The cat!" they chanted. They were a depraved audience eager to watch every reddened stripe of flesh that promised to blossom across my back during the impending lashes.

The fact that that little bastard Larry had been able to so nonchalantly slip out of this situation by merely finishing a taco made my blood boil. It made me so angry that it eclipsed the extreme reluctance I felt toward taking the only action I really had available to me at the moment. I really didn't want to leave 1885 with a new business opportunity left hanging, but I also have a personal policy against allowing myself to get flogged.

"Listen, gentlemen," I said. "This has all been one great big misunderstanding."

I added one of those nervous laughs tourists give when they realize they've overstepped their bravado in the wrong part of town. This was no mean feat, because the tendons straining in my left shoulder were sending signals to my brain that were not of the 'laugh' variety.

"Just what is it I've misunderstood?" said the first mate. The breeze shifted, and I became acutely aware that he smelled just as ugly as he looked.

"It's a funny thing really," I said, drawing things out as my left thumb found the right knob on the watch. "I was never really here."

I triple-clicked the watch's crown, activating the default emergency escape setting, and flashed right out of 1885 forever. Normally I try not to use my method in front of witnesses, but this was an acceptable deviation. No one was going to believe this bunch's story of how they all stared in wonder as the new crewman they were about to haze suddenly disappeared into nothingness. There was minimal risk that any of those goons would be able to use the experience to disrupt the timestream.

Still, I wasn't particularly looking forward to what I was flashing into. The default emergency escape setting jumps straight to the Cross-Time Coordination Agency Headquarters. In any case, I had a professional obligation to file a report on Larry. Communication with the CTCAHQ was definitely called for. But generally I like to bury a note a few years upstream and let them find it on their own. Face to face dealings with bureaucracy are not my strong point. I only hoped they would be more concerned with appearance of a new, undisciplined, random time traveler than they would be by my actual presence on the CTCAHQ campus.

CTCAHQ, AND I DO PRONOUNCE that like I'm bringing up phlegm, has their headquarters in what looks like a giant plastic eyeball on stilts overlooking the Olduvai Gorge. It's about ten stories high, fifteen if you count the stilts, with the middle five floors an open floorplan office monstrosity. Those five floors are crescent-shaped galleries affording every desk a view through the giant window of the iris. The building has no stairways or elevators, just a set of long curving ramps that switchback along the retina wall and connect to different levels unpredictably. Above and below the iris are the more sensitive departments of CTCAHQ.

Unless you're there, in the time of chimpanzees, you won't find it. The building doesn't exist in any other timeframe, so don't bother looking. It sits safely two million years in the past, at the dawn of humanity. The official line is that this is the best placement of headquarters because it's the perfect spot to protect humanity from a nihilistic rogue time traveler intent on destroying the human race before it even gets started. Honestly, I think they chose the time and place because the weather's fantastic. It's practically a resort atmosphere.

One of the more frustrating architectural quirks of the building is, no matter how hard you try to fine-tune your approach, visitors always arrive on the entrance mat. The entrance mat is a platform cantilevered out from the central floor and into the focal point of the eyeball. There's no way to unobtrusively slip in and make a report without every-damn-body in the Agency knowing you're there.

And, to make things just a little bit more annoying, the floor covering on the entrance mat is the same as the old carpet from the Portland International Airport. I have no idea why, but it makes every trip to CTCHAQ feel like stepping into a hashtag.

So, there I was, arriving on the entrance mat with great-great grandpa's watch in my hand and a strong desire for some prescription strength pain relievers. Not only did my shoulder ache from where I had been dangled, but I could really use something to take the edge off. I felt a building *ennui* at the thought of dealing with the kind of people who have no problem wearing formfitting cerulean jumpsuits.

Everyone working at CTCAHQ wears a cerulean jumpsuit. They say it's because the color reduces chronometric friction. I'm skeptical. I'm skeptical of any group of people over the age of five who dress up in matching pajamas.

Just off the entrance mat I saw my first CTAHQ jumpsuit. It was filled with a particularly uptight agent named Hastings. Early on in my solo career, Hastings had taken it upon himself to be a personal thorn in my side. Whenever one of my business activities veered even remotely close to the grayer areas of the Laws of Time, Hastings would be there to bust my balls.

With a smarmy, crap-eating grin.

Just like now.

"Greetings, Ishmael."

Smarmy...

...crap-eating...

...grin.

And I'll be damned if his jumpsuit didn't have white piping and epaulets now. I regretted my earlier haste. Re-growing the skin on my back would have been much preferable to being in the same building with these fashion-impaired timecops.

I managed to grunt a response at Hastings.

"Likewise, I'm sure," said the cerulean-clad prick. "I would say that it's a pleasant surprise to see you. But, to be honest, it's not. The Orb had placed my meeting your arrival on the day's duty roster. Neither pleasant nor a surprise, actually."

"No surprises in the CTCAHQ," I said.

"Please don't spit, Ishmael," he said. "We must set a good example for the hominids." He pointed out a vast circular window, the iris of the crazy eyeball building, to a family of hairy proto-humans lounging in the lush greenery nearby.

"Try just a little bit harder, Hastings," I said. "I can almost smell that smug sense of superiority you're trying to exude."

"This way," he said. "The Orb wants to debrief you personally."

The Orb. That was another guy who really creeped me out. Basically, in time traveler circles, anyone who has given up their actual name for an aggrandized combination of a noun and a definite article is someone to watch out for. Some of them can be pretty interesting, some of them downright fun, but the Orb...

Let's just say that time spent with the Orb does not come in doses small enough for my liking.

Hastings led me through long, looping ramps and corridors to the Orb's office. Along with my reluctance toward any conversation that can be described as a 'debriefing,' the architecture itself was messing with me. No corners anywhere and all the surfaces gradually curving into each other wherever they meet. The place always gives me vertigo.

"Any chance we could stop by the infirmary for some Dramamine?"

"Sorry," said Hastings, "but you're not on the Agency health plan."

"There's and agency health plan?"

"If you'd come to the fortnightly public meetings you would know these things."

"Does anyone else come to these meetings?"

Hastings' face wrinkled. I took his lack of an answer for a no. We walked in silence the rest of the way through those polished, organic, ramping hallways.

After some time, we reached the apex of the eyeball-shaped building, the severely acute angle of the exterior wall implying a shallow dome. Half the dome was taken up by a reception area furnished with the height of 1960's post-modern uselessness. Chairs in which it was impossible to sit upright and tables with legs that seemed to be designed based on conic sections spun at random angles. Cerulean shag carpeting. A bee-hived receptionist sitting at a desk formed from an S-shaped curve of Lucite.

Hastings led me right past the receptionist, through one of those science fiction dilating doors and into the darkened, secluded chamber from which the Orb kept track of all of time.

The Orb sat behind his desk, creepy and intimidating. He had a head the size of a prize watermelon and the ability to actually see time flowing around him. If he looked hard enough, and in the right direction, he could see the very ripples in the continuum as travelers pop in and out of the stream. He could figure out where a person had been and where they were going just by staring at them. It's a neat trick, and one that he'd parlayed into a nice upper management position. But he was a very unsettling guy to be around. He knew everything everyone around him was about to do before they did it. The only thing he didn't know was why.

I really hoped he wasn't expecting me to answer 'why' questions.

"Good epoch, Ishmael," said the Orb. I don't care what the appropriate butt-kissing protocol is, I wasn't going to respond to that ridiculously stilted, elitist salutation in kind.

"Sure. Good whatever," I said.

"A good *epoch* to you, sir," said Hastings, a man who adheres to ridiculous butt-kissing protocols like superglue.

"Go away, Hastings," said the Orb.

"Right away, sir."

"Leave!" shouted the Orb.

I have to admit, I really enjoyed hearing Hastings get yelled at. Maybe an audience with the Orb wouldn't be so bad after all.

As my eyes adjusted to the dark, I realized, no, this *would* be bad.

The Orb's head had grown since the last time I'd graced CTCAHQ. It was now the size of a Pilates ball. His office chair was rigged with a system of architectural scaffolding on which his head rested. His hair was so thin, due to his scalp being stretched over the enormity of his cranium, that it seemed a shame that it hadn't been shaved off entirely. But, then again, that was a tremendous amount of surface area to drag a razor across. Just looking at the giant bulb of his head, with his tiny face seated at its bottom corner, set off another round of vertigo within me.

"What brings you here, Ishmael?" the Orb said.

"Oh, I had a little complication," I said, trying to figure how best to word things so as not to accidentally pin any more responsibility on myself as necessary. Flashing out of the middle of a violent mob is something that, technically, the CTCAHQ frowns on. Too many witnesses.

As it was, I ended up giving the Orb an unembellished account of Larry and how he didn't even realize he had been traveling. Not even in the end, when he rediscovered his method in that awful taco he found in the breast pocket of his flannel shirt.

"I mean, who eats coelacanth?" I concluded. "The main reason these fish were lost to zoology for so long was that they are not good eating. Madagascar fishermen have been throwing the ugly suckers back in the ocean for millennia. Whenever they get hauled up in the nets, it's like, dammit, not this thing again."

"Agreed," said the Orb. "Our chef keeps putting it on the menu here for some reason. It's truly awful and I usually take the vegetarian option those days. But I might suggest tacos to him. It could be that the seasoning is the secret."

"It's your funeral," I said, relieved that the tone of the debriefing had turned conversational.

"Yes, funerals," said the Orb. "So many funerals..." His eyes rolled aimlessly in his tiny face as he waited for just the right moment to drop the other shoe on me. "Which reminds me. This Lawrence is far too dangerous to be allowed to stumble through the timestream unsupervised. Hand me your watch."

"What?" I said.

"Hand me your watch," said the Orb. "Or do I need to call Hastings in here to manhandle it from you?"

Reluctantly, I turned it over. The Orb took the watch and held it to a place on his forehead a foot and a half above his left eyebrow. The watch and the forehead began to glow with the same cerulean color as the timecops' jumpsuits. Several minutes of this glow, and a progression of positively inhuman facial expressions, passed before the Orb returned my watch.

"I'm deputizing you as Lawrence's chaperone," he said. "I believe you'll find him in San Diego."

"Hold on!" I said as the Orb, and the entire CTCAHQ building, dissolved around me, my objection echoing into the nothingness of an involuntary time jump.

The thing I hated most about the Orb was that, in any conceivable situation where you had to interact with him face to creepy little face, you were no longer in any position to make a choice about your fate. I suddenly, clearly identified the last moment I had anything resembling a choice in all of this: the first mate and his cat o' nine tails. I really could have made a different choice. I really could have made the choice to stay on the *Dogturd* and face the mate's lashings. That would have been a finite and transitory bit of pain that I would, in time, overcome. I'm a strong man. It was pride, really, that led me to bug out before the lashes came down. Pride in my ability to keep my ass from getting beaten. I could have made a different choice if it weren't for pride. And now an entirely different part of my pride was injured. Pride in my capacity as a free agent in a world where most people are imprisoned in lives prescribed for them by forces beyond their control.

I had lived outside of all that for quite a while. I had known the freest of all free wills. Not even time could hold me down. Because I had always had the freedom to avoid true consequences and responsibility. And now, one stupid choice...

Who am I kidding? It was the way it had to go down. The Orb would have dragooned me one way or the other. Still, a part of me was beginning to regret that I hadn't made a different choice.

Chapter 4
The Laws of Time

THE ORB HAD DONE ME the courtesy of sending me off to join my new 'apprentice' without so much as giving me a chance to negotiate the terms of the contract. That's the Orb, for you.

The CTCAHQ building melted way as the majority of human history played out before me. Some time travelers like to close their eyes, to look away, to pretend they step gingerly between one timepoint and another, ignoring the fundamental contiguity of the entire timestream. Believe me, it can be a lot easier on the stomach that way. Also, some are a little disheartened to watch as everything humanity has ever built inevitably crumbles and decays. Admittedly, that is a sobering image to take in. But that's just life run at fast forward. If you don't see that going down at normal speed, you're in serious denial, and you might miss something important.

Not always, but sometimes, I catch some little detail, an artifact, a plant, a valuable fossil in the making, that I'll be able to track down later. Usually, I like to dig them up at a point in time where I can make a tidy profit.

This time, however, I was too irritated with the Orb and his method of being a megalomaniacal control freak, that I was having trouble picking out the details. The best I could do was observe as the nearby tribe of homo habilis proto-people evolved before my eyes, crossed oceans and continents, fought wars and built empires, fell in love and fell to betrayal by their lovers, the whole human experience. I was caught up with a tiny group of them, that splintered off from the lines of kings and explorers, to fall through the cracks of civilization and arrive at the fallen state of grunge rockers crashed on a love seat and a couple couches in a crappy California apartment.

Larry's crappy California apartment.

"Dude!" said Larry, "What a trip! Come on in, bro."

I stepped through what was left of the screen door and into the fug of delayed pre-adult rock and roll lifestyle. To be fair, I'd seen worse dumps. When you travel the centuries and the continents you see some things. For instance, the place was quite a step up from anything you'd see on any given day in Haiti. However, considering this was one of the most privileged population demographics, the white male, in one of the most privileged habitats, California, during one of the most privileged decades, the 1990s, that humankind has ever known, the place was a total shithole. Whoever was actually held the lease on that apartment was definitely not getting their security deposit back.

Somewhere beneath a layer of cigarette butts, fast food wrappers, and empty beer bottles there was a floor. And on that floor was a carpet so badly stained it would take a team of chemical engineers to determine the color. There was a TV humming in the corner bathing the room in the cathode ray glow of Nintendo sprites dancing across its screen. Band flyers and centerfolds were stapled to lumpy walls that belied many a fist-sized dent. One dent in the drywall was actually a full body impression, embellished in sharpie with Mongoloid facial features and a word balloon calling 'Who took my POGs, muthafucka?'

"Larry," I said, "we need to talk."

"When'd you get to the party?" he said.

"This is a party?" I said, looking at the five dudes gathered around a Super Nintendo.

"It was righteous, dude," said the guy holding controller A.

"So many babes," said controller B. "We had to, like, say, 'ladies, please, three at a time's all I can handle.'"

"And let me guess," I said. "They all politely left about an hour ago so you sausages could play Madden '93?"

"Sure," said Larry. "These guys are the biggest frickin' liars in the world. Jeff says he's going to see Nirvana in Copenhagen. But we all know he's really going to Yuma to dig his mom a new sewer pipe."

"Don't talk about my mom like that," said Jeff. "And I'm going to Copenhagen."

"I'd save your money," I said.

"You don't like Nirvana, dude?"

"Love 'em. Just something tells me that leg of the tour's not going to happen."

"Fuck you, grizzled cob nobbler of little faith. I'm going to Nirvana."

This asshole was spouting the fake grunge slang the New York Times had unintentionally reported as an actual thing when everyone was scrambling to get any kind of info on the exploding Seattle music scene. The paper had been punked by someone who picked up the phone at an indie record label. She blithely told the reporter whatever nonsense popped into her head. That Times article was one of my personal favorite artifact of pop culture history. I just didn't realize anyone had actually picked up the fake slang and started using it. These guys were going to be heartbroken come April 5th.

"Suit yourself," I said. "If you want, I know a great travel agent. Cheapest flights around, but she only takes cash."

"Let me get back to you," he said.

I waded through the jetsam to where Larry sat. The loveseat didn't quite fit in the same living room with the two sofas the rest of the crew were perched upon. By its position, obstructing the apartment's hallway, it seemed a minor feat of athleticism might be necessary to hurdle the loveseat to get to the bathroom. And, from the dark, established stain on the arm furthest from Larry, I surmised that it was a feat often met in failure.

"Creeping Christ, you people piss on that thing?" I said.

"Dude," said player A, "the water's been shut off for a long time. What you going to do?"

"Right, when that happens it's best just to lie in your own filth," I said. "Larry, we got to get out of here."

"What's the rush?" he said. "I'm about to crash."

"Right there?" I said. "You've got a couple of couches, and you sleep on the piss loveseat?"

He shrugged.

"Larry," I said. "We need to get someplace with indoor plumbing. I've spent enough time in the 19th century for one evening."

"What's this 'we' stuff?" he said.

"The Orb has decreed, Larry."

"The herb has decreed?" he said. "Why didn't you say so? Let's jet."

Larry was obviously hearing what he wanted to hear. I didn't mind taking advantage of that.

What I did mind was that, as soon as we stepped out from the apartment and into the courtyard, I was face to face with Cross-Time Coordination Agent Hastings.

"Good evening, Ishmael," Hastings said, with the particularly smarmy grin that puts one in mind of the sort of person who enjoys watching others eat feces. "Long time, no see."

"Speak for yourself, Hastings," I said. "I just saw the Orb boot you from his office not more than an hour ago."

"How unpleasant for you," said Hastings.

I surmised that more time had passed for him, relatively, because his cerulean unitard was no longer adorned by epaulets. And the white piping had been replaced by triple stripes like you'd see on an Adidas track suit. CTCAHQ's standard protocol was to continually update their uniforms so people like me could never be quite sure when the hell they were coming from.

"How's the babysitting job going?" Hastings asked, smiling like he was the one helping himself to a spoonful of turds.

"Unpleasantly," I said. I choked back bile as it occurred to me that twice that day I'd been coerced into unpleasant chores on account of Larry. I mulled over which was worse, shoveling coal like a galley slave or chaperoning an oblivious newbie time traveler. Either one was way outside my preferred job description.

"This the guy with the herb?" Larry asked.

Hastings, you gotta love his charm, talked right over Larry as he said, "splendid. Let's walk and talk. This neighborhood gives me hives."

"Whatever you say, officer."

I wanted to put some quick distance between us and that 400 square-foot urinal Larry's friends called an apartment.

"This guy's a cop?" asked Larry.

"In a manner of speaking," said Hastings.

"This is a harsh realm," said Larry. "I thought we'd be swingin' on the flippity-flop, and now you go and narc on me."

"Relax, Larry," I said. "He's not that kind of cop. And I didn't realize anyone actually ever said 'swingin' on the flippity-flop.'"

"Absolutely," said Larry. "I read it in the New York Times, and they don't make stuff like this up."

"Spoken like a true lamestain, Larry." I turned to Hastings. "You can't be checking up on me already. What are you here for?"

"An adjacent investigation," he said, as we walked further from the land of two story, stuccoed apartment complexes and into a light industrial area closer to the waterfront.

"Hey," said Larry. "I know this place. That taco guy is around here."

"That taco guy," said Hastings, "has been flaunting his disrespect for the Laws of Time."

THE LAWS OF TIME ARE a funny set of limitations on time travel. Some of them are natural laws, and some are more like a gentleman's agreement among a select set of time travelers. A gentleman's agreement rigorously forced onto the rest of us by the boys and girls in cerulean, otherwise known as the Agency.

Or, as I like to call them, CTCAHQ. It's a simple anagram for Cross-Time Coordination Headquarters and every time I say it I get a chance to clear my throat and spit at the nearest one of them. I love these guys that much. Especially Hastings. One or two of them are all right. The Orb scares the living bejesus out of me with his creepy beach ball head. Then there's Agent Lovejoy. Let's just say a visit from Agent Lovejoy is never altogether terrible. She may be a timecop, but she's actually a decent human being. And she knows how to rock a cerulean unitard.

More about her later. We're talking about the Laws of Time, remember?

There are some Laws of Time that you just can't break no matter how hard you try. Like, you can't accidentally set in motion a chain of events that results in you never having been born. It's part of the Law of the Conservation of Time. Time is somehow part of living things, or living things are part of time, and the life cycles just don't wrap around themselves like that. It's like trying to push together the north poles of two very strong magnets. Try as you might, you can't get them together and they just flip themselves around the right way. There's actually some very intimidating looking mathematical equations that back this up. I've seen them, I don't understand them, but they are definitely some serious math.

Then there's the Law of the Conservation of Personality, also known as Marty's Law. This is one of the gentleman's agreement variety. In a nutshell, you don't cross your own timeline to give yourself privileged information about the future. At the inaugural meeting of the Cross-Time Coordinating Agency, this law was agreed to unanimously and without much discussion. Almost everyone at that first meeting had tried, at least once, to cross their own timeline in order to arrange complicated, and doomed, sexual liaisons for their younger selves... or even *with* their younger selves. It turns out that the human brain just isn't built to be able to objectively observe its own naked body doing naked things that said brain is not directly involved in doing, even if that brain is already engaged in doing other naked things with the naked body it's currently residing in. The difficulty of even trying to parse a sentence like that, let alone utter it in a public setting, prompted the Congress to move for an immediate vote with no discussion.

There are other laws, like the Law of Anachronistic Technology and the Law of Nondisclosure, that actually deserve to be enforced sometimes. Sometimes they can be discreetly and harmlessly skirted. Why not bring a Taser to a sword fight? If it can save you some time, and you're dressed like a crazy wizard, I say, go for it. Myths and legends come from somewhere, right? And if it helps you turn a tidy profit with minimal impact to historical events, what's the harm?

CTCAHQ is inclined to disagree with me on that one, but that's no surprise. It suits me to disagree with them most of the time.

At the moment, though, the question foremost in my mind was which of the Laws had the taco guy violated? And could these violations be redressed? And, if so, once these offending tacos were out of the equation, could CTCAHQ quickly establish a non-traveler status for Larry so that I could go back to my primary business of turning a tidy profit while discreetly skirting the Laws of Time?

"WHY ARE YOU LETTING us tag along on your bust?" I asked Hastings.

"We need to set an example for our new colleague," he said, almost chewing the word 'colleague,' into some sort of shape that might fit into his sentence. It didn't quite work, but I was at a loss to figure out a better descriptor for Larry, myself.

"Sure, sure." I said. "But what good's that at this point? The kid has no idea he's a time traveler."

"Guys," Larry butted in, "I hate to break it to you, but Comic-Con isn't for another six months. Nice Starfleet uniform, by the way."

He slapped Hastings on the shoulder, bro style.

"See what I mean?" I said.

"It's never too early to learn the consequences of trafficking in extinct animals," said Hastings.

I didn't buy it. Hastings disliked me equally as much as I disliked him. The Orb was probably putting him up to this, but why?

"Whatever," said Larry. "I see my taco guy. You two want something?"

In the parking lot of a corrugated steel warehouse, a solitary street lamp shined down on an old travel trailer and a picnic table. The trailer was decorated with the usual neighborhood graffiti and a menu board. An A-frame sign declared the special of the day: plesiosaur. I had been way off with my earlier assumption that the secret ingredient in Larry's special tacos was coelacanth.

"How does that work?" I asked Hastings.

Hastings, being a dick, didn't answer.

"I mean," I continued, "my watch can barely provide the method for moving myself and my clothes." (A deliberate understatement.) "If this taco guy managed to bring back an entire aquatic dinosaur, his method must draw a considerable amount of power."

By this time Larry had already made his way up to the window of the trailer and was ordering.

Hastings was still being a dick. He shoved Larry out of the way and started at the guy in the taco cart.

"Cease cooking and come quietly! You are under investigation for violating section 4.3 of the Laws of Time regarding the transport of foodstuffs across established epoch barriers!" Hastings was always one for sticking you with the letter of the law, if not the sense of it.

"What the fuck are you talking about, *pendejo?*" said the man in the taco truck.

Hastings pulled out his CTCAHQ credentials and barked, "where are you keeping your dinosaurs? Don't make me come in there!"

"Your friend's pretty intense," said Larry.

"He's not my friend," I said. "But, yeah. He could take it down a notch."

Larry and I were quite happy to watch the events unfold. We could both agree that Hastings was making a total ass of himself. He spent a good fifteen minutes trying to convince the taco guy that the CTCAHQ was actually a valid law enforcement agency. I was tempted to point out that Hastings, himself, was on the verge of flagrantly violating the Law of Nondisclosure when a new voice came out of a darkened corner of the parking lot.

"Put down your badge, Agent Hastings," the voice said. It was not a pleasant voice. "That man's only crime is not using separate cutting boards for meat and vegetables. Hardly your jurisdiction."

"And I should listen to you because?" said Hastings.

"Because," said the hulking, inhuman silhouette that belonged to the voice. "I get to decide how quickly, or how slowly, you die."

The silhouette was familiar to me, not because I'd ever traveled that far back in time, but because, as a kid, I'd spent hours poring over books on paleontology and begging my parents to take me to natural history museums. I knew all your major prehistoric megafauna and how to spell their multisyllabic names long before I entered the second grade. But still, there were obviously a few things I did not know about those fabulous thunder lizards. Like their conversation skills. I did not know that one.

"Would you fucking believe that?" said Larry. "A talking allosaur."

"No," I said, "I would not fucking believe that. But there it is."

Chapter 5

Dinosaur Problems

"DUDE," SAID LARRY. "I think Jeff must have roofied my Budweiser again."

"Sorry to harsh your realm, or whatever you grungies say, but this is really happening," I said.

What was happening was that a 30 foot long allosaurus wearing a monocle was eyeing Hastings the way a fat kid eyes a French fry. The allosaur had just explained to Hastings that death was most definitely on the evening's agenda. To the credit of his sky-blue uniform, Hastings didn't miss a beat in chiming in with his own agenda.

"Who are you?" said Hastings. "What are you doing here, and what did you put in those tacos?"

The allosaur let loose one of those maniacal laughs villains stay up late at night practicing. At least, judging from its body language, that's what I assume the allosaur's unholy vocalization was. It actually sounded more like a forklift dropping a stack of drywall in the middle of the aisle at Home Depot, but the effect was chilling.

Larry and I began a slow creep along the side of the taco stand, trying to keep as much of it between us and the dinosaur as possible.

"What makes you think I will tell you anything, little man," said the allosaur.

"It's not necessary, I'll admit," said Hastings. "I'd at least like to have a name to put on the report I'll have to file when I vaporize you."

As the giant, impossible dinosaur laughed again, I felt a new found appreciation for Hastings' giant, impossible cojones. How he was able to talk procedure while he was in the very real position of potentially being bitten in half I'll never know. Somewhere beyond the fight or flight instinct is the place where Hastings lives.

Larry and I, on the other hand, were decidedly on the same track of the instinct. We had almost backed our way around to the other side of the taco cart when I felt a hand on my shoulder.

"Where do you *pendejos* think you're going?"

It was the cook. He was pointing something toward us, perhaps a weapon. In the dark it was hard to see what, but given the situation, everything seemed menacing.

"Just looking for a cash machine," I stalled.

The cook laughed. A human laugh. The kind of laugh that comes from an uncle who has once again successfully executed the pull my finger gag.

"Homeboy already paid," he said, gesturing toward Larry. "Just didn't want you taking off without *su comida*."

"Right," said Larry. My tacos."

The object in the cook's hands turned out to be a paper bag soaked with the tell-tale grease spots of a legitimate taco joint.

"Just a minute," I said, snatching the bag from the cook. "What do you see going on over there with my friend in blue?"

"The health inspector?" said the cook. "He's talking with my boss, Jorge-George."

"And Jorge-George is..." I lead.

"A *pinche güero* who never comes to *this* part of town at night."

"Are you telling me you don't see the freaking dinosaur?" said Larry.

"Which party did you just come from?" he said. "All I see's a couple *cabrónes* fighting over how hot I keep my grill."

There was obviously some sort of perception filter at work. But which way was it filtering? I took out my watch, flipped up the crystal, and viewed the dinosaur through it. It was a mother verbing dinosaur, all right.

The allosaur was making even more thunderous laughing sounds as Hastings pulled out his citation book. It occurred to me that, like the cook, Hastings couldn't see through the filter either. And I was hit by the sudden ethical dilemma of whether I should help out an unwitting timecop. Nine times out of ten I'd be totally willing to let Hastings twist, but this time he was at a mortal disadvantage. I had a clean shot at running hell for leather to the nearest steel reinforced doorway, but I just couldn't do it. The opportunity to set Hastings up to owe me big time was just too great.

"All right, Larry," I said. "We need to come up with a distraction."

"Look," he said, "I don't even know that guy, but I did see Jurassic Park. If there's one thing I learned, it's that those things travel in packs."

"You're one thousand percent wrong," I said, easing my way toward a likely looking Suzuki Samurai on the street at the edge of the lot. "This is an allosaurus. The pack hunters in JP were velociraptors."

Somewhere in the night rang the sound of boxcars coupling, or was it other allosaurs laughing? I hated to admit that Larry could be right.

I pulled a screwdriver, a hammer, and vice grips from the inner pocket of my coat. Yes, a trench coat. I like to carry a lot of tools.

"Here," I said to Larry, handing him the vice grips. "Let's do this."

"Do what?" said Larry.

"We're stealing a car," I said as I picked up the pace and headed toward the Suzuki.

"Okay," he said, matching my pace, and hopping into the ridiculously tiny sport vehicle alongside me. "But if we get pulled over, I'm just a hitchhiker. You don't know me."

"I *don't* know you," I said as I popped the screwdriver into the ignition and grabbed the vice grips from Larry. A little artfully applied leverage on the steering column, and the engine turned over on the first try.

Some more applied leverage, and the stolen micro-truck tore up over the curb and into the parking lot. I gunned it toward Hastings and the dinosaur.

"Wrong way, dude!" said Larry.

"We're going for broke," I said. "If things get bad, just eat one of your tacos."

"I lost my appetite."

We were heading straight for Jorge-George, the allosaurus, or whoever he really was. I wasn't entirely sure the Suzuki would even put a dent in him. After a moment's reflection on the vehicle's super light build, I was absolutely sure I wouldn't put a dent in Jorge-George. I cut the wheel and remembered why you don't cut the wheel on a Suzuki Samurai.

We must have rolled about five times before our little steel death crate skidded to an upside-down stop in front of Hastings.

"Holy spit!" he ejaculated. "Where did that dinosaur come from?"

Hastings is the kind of guy who, when he shouts something, it really is best described by the old-fashioned sense of the word 'ejaculate.' Also, he's pretty much a prick. Apparently our improvised car wreck had done the trick of shaking him out of the effects of the perception filter.

The dinosaur kicked the hood of the Suzuki and sent us for another quarter turn.

"I hope you can appreciate the seriousness of your position now, Hastings," said the allosaur.

"My position is always serious, Mr. Jorge-George, if that's even your real name," said Hastings. "You are in major violation of all regulations pertaining to cross-time transit of animal protein for comestible purposes. I would like to see your permits."

"And I," said Jorge-George, "would like to bite your head off."

The allosaur now had one foot on the front bumper of the Suzuki and was rocking it ever so slightly.

Larry and I swayed, still belted into the little death trap. As my senses came to me, I could hear a quick drip, drip, drip and smell the sickly sweet odor of spilled gasoline.

"This really, really, sucks a big one," whispered Larry.

"You still got those tacos?" I asked.

"How can you think of eating at a time like this?"

The allosaur took a step toward Hastings. The creature was dragging his left foot and limping tenderly. The Suzuki must have done some damage after all.

"This is bigger than you, Hastings," said the allosaur. "It's bigger than the Cross-Time Coordinating Agency, and it's bigger than your arbitrary, human Laws of Time."

"Not all of them are arbitrary," said Hastings. I could see him patting his unitard looking for something. He was probably searching for his method trigger. He was out of his depth and needed to flash back to CTCAHQ. Losing track of his time travel device was very un-Hastings-like.

"We've got to get out of this micro-truck," I said to Larry. "It's leaking gas like a busted-up micro-truck."

"Right," said Larry, popping the seatbelt latch, tumbling onto his head and into the parking lot.

I braced myself with my arm, and I still had a hell of a time getting out without pressing my face directly into the asphalt. It was not a glorious evening. I grabbed the bag of tacos and slithered out of the wreckage in the growing pool of gasoline.

The allosaur, Jorge-George, was backing Hastings up against the wall.

Hastings was sweating through his unitard.

I wished I'd had a camera. What I did have was a hammer. At twenty yards it's not too hard to huck a hammer at a dinosaur and hit him. With a little bit of finesse you can huck it right at his injured left leg. With a lot of finesse, I discovered, you can piss the dinosaur off enough that it starts chasing you instead of the guy he's got backed up against a taco cart.

"That's right, you anachronistic son of a bitch! Come and get me!"

What was I saying? In retrospect, I chalk it up to the gas fumes. I was running again, and Larry was running with me. I suppose Larry wasn't as dumb as I'd given him credit for. Of course, how smart do you need to be to run away from a dinosaur?

We'd gotten halfway to the edge of the parking lot when Jorge-George stopped chasing us, and turned back to Hastings. Hastings was still frantically searching for his method.

"Do you think he's looking for this?" Larry asked. He held up a metal cylinder about the size of a small flashlight. It was lined with several rows of tiny buttons and flashing LEDs.

"That's totally what he's looking for," I said.

"I boosted it from him on the walk over," said Larry. "It looked like something that would be cool to take to Laser Floyd."

"Larry," I said, "on any other day I'd buy you a drink for pulling a stunt like that. But, today, Hastings is totally screwed."

Jorge-George was now positioned directly over the desperate Hastings, looking very much like he was intending to literally screw the timecop before eating him.

"I'm not sure I can watch this."

The dinosaur's jaw hinged open and moved in towards Hastings. Hastings didn't scream or flinch, but turned to look directly into the gaping maw of the carnivore.

Just then, the Suzuki's gas tank finally exploded. The concussion from the blast was enough to send the dinosaur jerking out of his crouch. Larry saw the opportunity and took it.

"Hastings!" he shouted as he threw the metal cylinder, the trigger to Hastings' method, his time machine, if you will. We all watched as the cylinder followed Newton's laws along a very hopeful looking arc. However, just as it's easy to throw a hammer at a dinosaur and hit your target, it proved very difficult to do the same with Hastings' trigger. It fell five feet short, and on the wrong side of Jorge-George.

Another horrific dinosaur laugh, like stacks of metal filing cabinets tumbling down the Pyramids of Giza, sounded as Jorge-George moved in for the kill.

Chapter 6
Lovejoy

EVERYBODY'S TIME TRAVEL method, their device or trigger or process that sends them time travelling, is different. As far as I can tell, no research has ever gone in to figuring out why that is. Or, if anyone has researched it, they aren't telling. One of the central tenants of the Cross-Time Coordination Agency's rulebook is that knowledge of time travel would be way too dangerous for everyone involved if governments ever got a hold of it. A whole section of Agents is dedicated to convincing governments that pursuing time travel is a colossal waste of resources. As a result, quality research institutions never get involved in time travel because there is absolutely no grant money at stake. So, the question of why my method was a watch, while Larry's was somehow triggered by dinosaur tacos, and Agent Hastings' method was wrapped up in an aluminum tube the size of a couple double A batteries lined end to end, would probably never be answered.

And, honestly, at the moment I didn't really care.

What I didn't want to see was Hastings get bitten in half by an allosaurus. As much as Hastings gets on my nerves, I didn't actually want to see him dead. I just, generally, didn't want to see him.

But there we were in this dark, industrial parking lot with Hastings cornered against a taco cart and said dinosaur bearing down on him like an amorous giraffe preparing to mount a donkey. Larry had tried, and failed to throw the lightweight cylinder to Hastings. The pass came up short and things looked very, very bad.

"That guy is so screwed," said Larry.

"And we're screwed next," I said.

"Why doesn't the dinosaur just eat him and get it over with?" said Larry.

"Larry," I said, "when did you get smart?"

He had a point.

"That allosaur's after something. And, despite his suggestive posture, I don't think it's sexual."

"It totally looks like he's going to go for it though," said Larry.

"It may appear so," said another voice, British, female, and carrying just the right timbre to set my heart atwitter, "but I'm afraid human anatomy and dinosaur cloacae just aren't compatible in any meaningful way."

"Hello, Lovejoy," I said.

I didn't turn, I didn't move. I didn't dare turn my eyes because, as much adrenaline as I had pumping through me right then, I couldn't risk catching a glimpse of the superlative way my favorite timecop made the cerulean CTCAHQ unitard work.

Larry, wasn't so prepared.

"um... hi," he said.

"Right," said Lovejoy. "It seems our saurian friend is trying to get Hastings to emergency default back to headquarters so he can trace the destination coordinates."

"I hate emergency default," I said. Emergency default is what got me saddled as Larry's time travel chaperone. If I could set the emergency default in my watch for my favorite bar in my favorite year, I would do it. But it's locked on CTCAHQ just like everyone else's. When you get in too tight of a jam and have to blindly flash out of a situation, you have to explain yourself to the Orb. Not like he doesn't already know what's going on. He just likes to stare at you from the tiny face in his colossal head and watch you squirm. I really, really hate emergency default.

"Of course you would," said Lovejoy. "You break the law."

"Only when following it is inconvenient," I said. "The rest of the time I abide." I flashed her a rakish grin.

A rakish grin? What was I doing trying to flirt with her? It's a dead end street, but I always take it.

Meanwhile, the allosaur was still pawing at Hastings, as Hastings stoically composed himself. The stand-off no longer looked like a tableaux from the adult's only section of a sci-fi convention's silent art auction.

"I'm totally defaulting on my student loans," said Larry.

"Lawrence," said Lovejoy," you have no idea what we're talking about. So, do shut up."

It made me want to flirt with her more, but business was at hand, and, like usual, the sexiest thing I could actually do is start taking care of it.

"He's not going to be able to default," I said. "His trigger's two yards away from him on the wrong side of the dinosaur." I pointed at the cylinder lying in the lot.

"Bugger," said Lovejoy. "There's an elaborate ambush for that dinosaur waiting at HQ." She sighed. "Looks like it's time for Plan B." The unmistakable sound of a heavy energy weapon being warmed up hit my ears. I turned to see her shouldering a 22nd Century fusion plasma rifle.

"What about the Law of Anachronistic Technology?" I asked.

"That law's rather inconvenient at the moment. Wouldn't you agree?" She winked at me.

Dammit, why'd she always have to turn the charm on right when it would be the most opportune moment for me to leave. Her holding that portable cannon was one thing. Winking at me, though, guaranteed that I would have to stick around and see this thing out. If it ended smoothly, there was a chance for drinks later.

"All right," shouted Larry. "Set phasers for kill!"

The dinosaur turned toward us.

"Well, that's done it for the element of surprise," said Lovejoy, bearing her weapon on the allosaur.

"Horkachorge," she addressed the beast, "we seem to be at a bit of an impasse here."

So its name was Horkachorge, not Jorge-George. Made sense. I guess. I don't know how dinosaur names work, but I was pretty sure Spanglish wasn't the common root.

"How is this an impasse?" asked the dinosaur. "From my perspective, I'm getting everything I want."

"Are you, now?" said Lovejoy. "Is one of the things that you want a grapefruit sized piercing in the tail? Because I can start off with that."

Horkachorge whipped his entire body around and took two steps toward us. The great arc of his tail swung across the parking lot, catching Hastings across the mid-section.

Hastings hit the pavement again.

"You don't know who you're dealing with, Agent Lovejoy," said the thunder-lizard, with actual thunder in his voice.

"Doesn't matter," said Lovejoy, shifting her rifle and firing a blast at the nearby overturned Suzuki Samurai. The remains of the micro-truck burst into a shower of white hot shrapnel that sprayed across the other end of the parking lot.

The dinosaur coolly glanced at the wreckage and then turned toward Lovejoy.

"Impressive toy," he said. Then suddenly he pointed behind us with his tiny allosaur arm. "Hey! Is that Paul McCartney?"

That really shouldn't have worked, but for some reason it did. We all turned and looked, just long enough for the dinosaur to scoop up Hastings from the pavement. Now, with hostage in hand, the dinosaur loped toward the darkness on the other end of the lot.

"You two," said Lovejoy. "Steal us another car."

"I'd love to," I said, "but my tools are kind of scattered at the moment."

"Take this," she said, and tossed something toward me. It was a universal key fob remote. And by universal, I mean universal. It would start anything.

As I looked around at our options, Lovejoy gave chase on foot. She was losing ground fast, seeing as she was pursuing a bipedal reptile. She fired a few blasts to try and rein the beast in as best she could, but the thing was fast.

The closest car at hand was a 4-door Malibu, 1982-ish. Larry complained immediately, calling it a 'grandma hoopty.'

"We don't have time to be picky," I said, popping the door locks by pressing a button on the fob. "Get in back. I've got a feeling Lovejoy's going to want shotgun."

"Lase shotgun," said Larry, pulling the door closed behind him.

The Malibu sputtered to life. I was none too concerned with modeling responsible driving for my protégé. The tires squealed and laid down some nice streaks of rubber as we joined the chase.

I brought the car alongside Lovejoy, and, without losing a step, she hopped inside. Rather than bother with leaning out the side window like a character from the Dukes of Hazzard, she blasted out the windshield and rested her rifle on the dash.

We were quickly making headway on the dinosaur. The gap between us and him closing as the parking lot's pavement disappeared and gave way to gravel. The Malibu lurched and slid as we changed surfaces, but so did the dinosaur. He only had one direction he could go as the long, unbroken wall of a warehouse hemmed him in.

It didn't last, though. At the end of the warehouse, the dinosaur tore off to the right, and into further shadows. The Malibu took the corner like a stock racecar, and we quickly pulled alongside the dinosaur as it began following a rail spur that butted against another warehouse.

Lovejoy shouted at the out of time allosaur.

"Are you ready to come peacefully?"

Horkachorge screamed with a voice that sounded like an oncoming freight train. Or was it the sound of the actual oncoming freight train? There was an actual freight train ahead of us. It was hard to tell which was making the sound. It could actually have been both. Who could tell?

Horkachorge hurled Hastings onto the hood of the car and leaped. His powerful saurian legs lifted right up to the roof of the warehouse, right out of the way of the actual train bearing down on us and blowing its horn.

I cut the wheel and pulled us to a stop away from the tracks. The allosaur was gone with no hope of explanation.

I was finally able to look up at Hastings where he had landed on the hood of the car. He looked like he had aged 40 years in the last few minutes. More than looked it. He had a beard, gray hair, a sweat shirt and yoga pants instead of the sky-blue jumpsuit he had been wearing earlier.

He actually had aged 40 years. It appeared that some sort of screwed up timecop life insurance plan was at work. Hastings had been in an inevitable mortality situation, but rather than let him die like any decent employer would, the Orb plucked him out of his timeline and returned an older, more decrepit version.

Slowly, painfully, Hastings turned his to me. His eyes widened.

"You," he said. "You... You!"

"I what?" I said.

"You *would* have to be here," Hastings gasped. "You son of a..." His voice trailed off as the light went out from his eyes.

"Well," said Lovejoy. "On top of the rest of this mess, that's definitely put me off my breakfast."

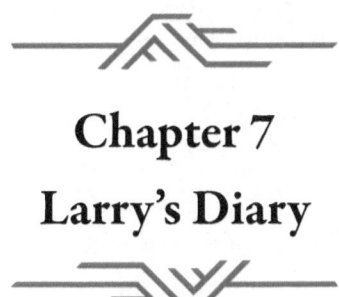

Chapter 7
Larry's Diary

SO, LIKE, I DON'T KNOW how to do this. What is this, high school? Ishmael says it's good practice to keep some kind of diary, so you can you know keep track of when you are, but I think that's some kind of bullshit. I never see him write anything down.

On the other hand, I can't remember half the shit that happened since that dinosaur killed Hastings by, like, turning him a hundred years old, or something. Apparently I time travel when I eat tacos now. It used to have to be special tacos made out of time-traveled dino-fish meat. Now it's just about any kind, except for those crappy chain restaurants. All they do is give me the shits, like always.

Ishmael tells me I need to clean up my language because I'm supposed to be representing to a whole other... shit, I can't remember why he wants me to clean up my language. Probably because he's an asshole.

Anyway, it feels like it's been a couple months since Hastings got wasted. That was pretty harsh. And that one really hot timecop, Lovejoy, told us to get the fu-, excuse me, hell out of there before the dust had time to, you know, stop hanging in the air. So, that was too bad, because Ishmael was right. She totally does wonders for that Starfleet outfit the timecops wear.

Anyway, we haven't seen her, or any other timecops since.

Which is pretty okay, because, cops, right? But, still. Hot timecops are another thing, right?

Ishmael's been showing me the ropes of being a time traveler. He's got this watch thing, that takes him places, or times, or whatever. He says he's borrowing it from his great great grandpa, or something. He can dial it, and set it for specific points like historically awesome concerts (keep pushing for a trip to Altamont and keep getting denied). It also has a bunch of futuristic tri-corder things it does, like detects stuff that's in the wrong time, and, you know, points out hidden dinosaurs and crap like that. And it has this thing that he says is like an eye-pod, but when I asked him "what the fawk's an eye-pod?" he just laughed at me. Asshole.

For some reason having to do with some timecop bullshit, wherever or whenever Ishmael guess to with his watch, I go there too. By the same token, whenever I eat a taco, my man Ishmael is taking a little trip as well. So, we're totally connected at the butt now, which is probably why Ishmael's even bothered to let me know some of the finer points of time travel.

Like, the timecops will really come down hard on your ass if you take an Uzi to medieval Florence.

Whatever. I still say those Borgia dicks had it coming, even if it did take a week to clean up the mess to CTCAHQ's satisfaction. Those fu—excuse me—effers.

Mostly Ishmael takes me to a bunch of places like you'd see in a history textbook, only the next town over and who gives a shit because nothing ever happened there. He says that's the safest way to travel. So far I've seen drafty taverns in three different centuries. The beer was pretty damn good, though, so I'm not complaining. Apparently, in the past, it was all kick-ass micro-brews. Not sure I'll even be able to swallow the old silver bullet by the time I get back to San Diego.

We go other places when I chow on a taco. Seems like fish tacos wind us up somewhere near the coast while chicken or beef take us further inland. The year seems to be totally up for grabs.

I thought Ishmael would shit a brick this one time when I had a machaca mini-chimi and suddenly we were surrounded by these Russian dudes in scary ass CCCP uniforms. I was thinking, oh shit, we're going to have to go all Red Dawn and fight our way out of this one, but Ishmael really pulled through. He spoke some Russian to them and, before I knew it, we were doing shots with these guys. They were even going to let me try shooting an AK, when this one guy with a crazy pushbroom mustache showed up and started yelling and shit.

Pretty soon Ishmael and I were naked in a jail cell somewhere underground in Russia. I was pretty sure that was where I was totally going to die. I mean, Ishmael was really about to beat the crap out of me for dragging him into Stalin-land and getting him separated from his watch. He had murder in his eyes, and without his clothes one, I could tell the dude had the muscles to do it. And a pretty respectable package. It was a very confusing moment.

And then I let out this machaca chimi burp, and for some reason that did the trick. We were the fu- the hell out of there, and back in my crappy apartment. And somehow we had our clothes and Ishmael had his watch back. Which was cool, because, one, Ishmael didn't want to kill me anymore, and, two, my roommates are total dicks. They would have given us all kinds of hell if we'd showed up there naked.

We had a couple other odd turns of the taco. Nothing too crazy. No talking dinosaurs, thank god. Who the hell knew dinosaurs could talk? There was some shit in France where all kinds of people were getting their heads cut off, but Ishmael knew this wine shop we could hang out in. The lady who ran the place knitted all the fricking time. It was crazy. All that knitting. Like, what the eff, right? The wine was all right. I've had better though. This was totally your 'two buck chuck' variety, which was kind of disappointing. You know, it was France, right. But I guess it was a bad year for France.

I think Ishmael is getting a little tired of these training missions, or whatever it is we're doing. He keeps bitching about how he'd like to get back to his business. When I ask what that is, he says 'import/ export.' That's bullshit. I'm pretty sure he's just a hobo. He certainly knows how to get people to buy him drinks, so that's awesome. We'll see if he actually has a business besides knowing which parties to crash.

He says I'm almost ready for something called chronocaching. He won't tell me what that is, though. He says I have to see it in action, and that's what we're doing tomorrow. Cool. Whatever. I guess I'm a time traveler now.

Chapter 8
Chronocaching 101

(ISHMAEL)

Larry and I have been laying low for a couple months. There are too many questions about the night Hastings died that I do not want to know the answers to. So far, so good. None of our friends from the CTCAHQ have peaked in on us since the Borgia Incident, which is just fine.

In the meantime, we've been poking and prodding around the edges of Larry's time travel method. And poke and prod as we may, whenever he goes I go. There's no fighting it. So I've resorted to teaching him some of the tricks of the trade.

I haven't worked with a partner for a long time. A long time. I don't necessarily like it, but I don't like resting on my laurels, either. There's too much to do, especially when you have the means to stop by any point in history to do it.

Today was a lesson in Chronocaching 101.

"It's like geocaching, except with time," I explained as we slipped through a gap in the cyclone fencing.

"What the fork is geocaching?" said Larry.

"Right," I said, "I keep forgetting you're from about ten years before technology really starts being worth a damn."

We were sneaking onto the construction site for a mixed use building, retail and condos. It was a still a few years before meth would become all the rage and any sort of loose copper would disappear job site before the foreman closed his lunchbox for the afternoon. It was quite possible that something useful to a certain someone I know in a later century might pop up.

"What are you talking about?" said Larry. "You saw my buddy's Super Nintendo."

"That's exactly what I'm talking about," I said. "That thing's not worth a damn."

My flashlight swept over the trenches lined with rebar that were destined to soon be entombed in concrete. This was going to work. Now to find the MacGuffin, the thing I could parlay into something personally worthwhile a few hundred years down the road.

"What are we doing here?" said Larry.

"We're trespassing," I said. "And we're looking for some durable goods with a minimum of moving parts. Tools of some sort might be good. Drop forged wrenches, maybe?"

"Oh, so we're stealing something?" said Larry.

"How can we be stealing?" I said. "Nothing we touch is going to leave this site for centuries."

"Really?" said Larry, kicking at the dirt. "That's kind of disappointing."

"That's just the first part."

"Ow!" said Larry, his foot connecting with something in the dark.

I swung my flashlight beam around to reveal a case of fourteen inch diamond saw blades. They were an off-brand, but even so they were something I could definitely barter with the Storemaster of Wal. Whatever idiot left them out in the open deserved to be fired.

"This is what we're looking for, Larry."

"Saw blades?"

"I know a guy. All we have to do is place them somewhere we can find them later on."

I took three of the blades and wrapped them in a metalized mylar bag. I tossed the bag at Larry. He almost fell into the rebarred trench next to him.

"Cheesus Crust, dude! Give a guy a heads up, why don't you?"

"Sure," I said. "Wedge that under some of the iron down there and throw some dirt on it."

Larry did a half-assed job of it, but, in truth, half-assed was all that's required.

"What's the point?" asked Larry.

"In a couple days it'll be covered in concrete, not to be disturbed until long after the collapse of civilization as you know it."

"Bullshit," said Larry.

"Watch your language," I said. "And watch this."

I hit the jump toggle on my great-great grandfather's pocketwatch.

TIME TRAVEL CAN BE a nice thing to watch when you have the luxury. Too often I find myself too pumped with adrenaline because I'm on the run from something. Dinosaurs. Robots. Stalin. It's always something. But this was one of those lovely moments at the start of a job where everything was going just right, and I could sit back and enjoy it.

The time jumps where you move chronologically, but not spatially, are the best. For just one moment everything happens at one time. Cities rise, collapse, and remake themselves. Forests recede and then reclaim the countryside. Concrete highways build themselves, then collapse, then are replaced by nothing but flowers. If you travel far enough, everything wrong that humans have done to a place gets erased. At first it's a little sad as the buildings crumble, but then it feels like a definite victory. And for the last part of that moment, where everything is everything at the same time, you definitely feel like the Buddha.

Unless you go through a stretch of volcanic activity. That pretty much rattles the nirvana out of you.

This time there were no volcanoes, only a significant swath of suburban Michigan reverting to boreal forest. I probably should have told Larry to bring a jacket.

IT WAS AUTUMN. CHILL and crisp the way autumns used to be. It was nice to know that only a couple hundred years after the Crash the harshest effects of global warming would run their course. The years of the Crash itself are a very scary place to go in very much the same way as you wouldn't want to visit London during a plague year. But afterwards, it's truly a new world. You need to watch out for dogs, though.

"Ishmael," Larry whined, "why didn't you tell me to bring a jacket."

"Because you should always bring a jacket. And you don't listen to me very often. Now, do you see where you stashed those saw blades?"

"Hunh?"

"The saw blades, Larry. It's time to retrieve them."

Larry looked around at the trees with in their fall colors, their trunks ripping asunder the blacktop of the parking lot that once spread at our feet.

"Where are we?" he asked.

"We're in the exact same spot we were before I hit fast forward on the world," I said. "You remember where you left the saw blades, don't you?"

"Shit," he said. "I don't know. I guess..." In front of us was a pile of rubble covered in decades' worth of decayed leaves and organic matter and looking not unlike a lovely mound of dirt. "Over in that, I guess."

"Here's a shovel," I said, handing him the collapsible camping spade I keep in my trench coat.

"Seriously?" he said. "They got buried in concrete. You think I can dig them out with this?"

"They were buried in concrete that's since sat out in at least a hundred years of acid rain with a couple hundred years of regular rain on top of that. It should be as easy as digging a cat turd out of the litter box."

I LIED. IT WASN'T. It took Larry about half an hour to dig out the chronocached diamond saw blades. While he was busy with that task, and trying very hard to stretch his expletive vocabulary beyond the confines of the f-bomb, I took a survey of our surroundings.

I'd been through this neck of the woods on other occasions. Fishing trips, mostly. There were some epic Nick Adams style fishing adventures to be had, even in the Lower Peninsula. Sure, you might want to check the fish for extra limbs, and the River Rouge was still a mess, but for the most part it was quite pleasant. So long as you bugged out by sundown.

A four lane stretch of pulverized Interstate highway lay in a mound that stretched from one break in the trees to another. Following it for a few miles would put us in range of the fortress-town of Wal. That's where we'd be doing some business. The locals were friendly, and they new quite a few ingenious ways of preparing venison. And they spoke a fashion of English that you could almost understand.

"Jeez, these are heavy," said Larry as he dragged the metalized mylar bag out of the trench he'd dug. The package truly hadn't aged a day. "Anything else need digging up?"

While Larry did have a number of negative qualities, he was a champion shovel man. I was a little amazed that he hadn't complained during his excavation. The kid deserved a reward.

"Larry," I said. "Have I told you about the amazing craft brewing tradition they have in Wal?"

"You mean, like espresso?" said Larry.

"Yegads, man," I said. "How narrow is your window on the world?"

"I went to public high school, dude," he said.

"I'm talking about beer, Larry. The kind of beer heroes drink in legends."

"I usually go with Coors or Rolling Rock," said Larry.

"I'm sure you do," I said. "Let's get moving. We want to get to Wal before sundown."

WE'D BEEN FOLLOWING the decayed highway for about an hour before I noticed we were being followed. It was hard to tell at first whether our shadow was man or beast. Then I caught a furtive glimpse of him when the road crossed a meadow and his cover was scarce. He was definitely a man, although there was something about his posture and his gait that belied a wildness reminiscent of the hominids who loiter near the CTCAHQ building in the time of chimpanzees.

He was probably harmless, I figured. Plus, we had saw blades and a collapsible camp shovel. We could do some damage if need be.

IT WAS ANOTHER HOUR before I realized we'd been going the wrong way. I would have cussed myself a blue streak, but I didn't want to let on to Larry that I'd made such a rookie move.

We stopped for a break while I considered our options. Doubling back while we had a tail on us could be fatal. The last thing you want to do when you're being followed is to give the appearance that you have no idea where you're going.

"Hoss," said Larry. "I gotta take a dump."

"Can it wait?" I said.

"For what?" he said. "A rest stop? We're in the forking woods at the end of the forking world."

"Fine," I said, keeping my eyes on the patch of greenery I'd last seen our follower lurking near. "Keep an eye out for dogs."

"uh," said Larry, "you got any T.P?"

LARRY WAS TAKING AN uncomfortable amount of time taking care of business. At least he was making a lot of noise doing it, so I knew he was all right. I concocted a plan to cut cross country and circle back to the highway in order to put us back in the right direction. The mild subterfuge probably wouldn't shake our tail, but it was sure to keep Larry from noticing we'd been going the wrong way.

When Larry emerged from his shit break I announced my intention to take a shortcut.

"Sure," said Larry. "So long as we're heading in the opposite direction from my turd mound."

As soon as we trekked ten yards from the highway, our tail revealed his scrawny, leather clad self. He practically jumped on top of us screaming and waving his arms madly.

"Murder! Murder and foreclosure! Evil freight-men there! Dogs over other there! And no Ditch Witch! Lies! Crud! Crud! Crud! Go no further! You're befucked!"

Like I said, the locals spoke a *kind* of English.

Chapter 9
Prelude to a Bigtime Clustercuss

(*Ishmael*)

But it was okay. I knew this guy. He was a bit of a smi-feral man-child, even by post-Crash standards, but he was essentially harmless. Larry looked a little spooked by him, though.

"Holla, Cooper" I said. "What else is news?"

"Murder," he said, his eyes twitching through the woods. "Murder two months thence. Murder two months hence. Hostile takeovers in the freight business. Bigtime clustercuss. I'm talking some serious Macbeth shit going on." Cooper wasn't your typical resident of this neck of the woods. Most people lived in tightly knit bands held together by ancient allegiances. When the Crash hit, the only people who made it out were the people who could trust each other with their lives. But where Cooper came from, no one is quite sure. What the people in Wal do know is that, when Cooper was a kid, someone found him sleeping in a chicken coop. It was noted that the chickens laid more eggs when he was there, so they let him stay.

And then one day I thought it would be fun to teach him how to read. The weird part is it took exactly one day, and I'm by no means a teacher. The kid was bright, but he was none too strong in the social graces.

To look at Cooper was to look at exactly what you'd expect out of a raving crazy living in the woods. Wiry. Wild-eyed. Knotted-hair. Clothed in tattered pelts and scavenged sheets of Tyvek. But he knew the trees and he knew the animals. He was the guy who could make it through the woods at night and not be torn apart by dogs and cougars.

"How does Wal fare?" I asked.

"The Storemaster said I could dine with his daughter if I got the job done."

"Sounds generous of him," I said.

"But there was murder and dogs and there wasn't any Ditch Witch to be found," said Cooper. "I had to return the freight and proffer a refund. I was near to half-befucked that day, but there was a calving later which I helped in and got paid some soup and a sleep in the barn."

"Who is this guy?" said Larry.

"This guy is Cooper," I said. "Cooper, meet Larry. He doesn't know anything."

"Doesn't surprise me," said Cooper, sniffing the air above Larry's shoulders. "Shshsh."

Cooper held his palm up, then flapped it for a moment, like the wing of a rock dove settling in to drop a turd on tombstone. He began pacing out a wide circle around us. His piercing gaze alternated between us and the surrounding woods.

"What's he looking for?" asked Larry.

"Everything, near as I can tell. Just let him do his thing."

At this response, Larry dropped his load of saw blades on the ground. The sudden noise made Cooper jump. He snapped his head straight toward Larry and showed his teeth.

"Double-you tee eff, man?" said Larry.

"You two shouldn't be out this way," said Cooper.

"I agree," I said. "Any chance you could get us to Wal by the quickest route."

"Well," said Cooper, "there's the road..."

"I know you know there's a better way than the road," I said. "The Storemaster is saving me some bacon. I can pay you to guide us."

"I don't have a license to work in Wal," he said.

"We're not in Wal," I said.

"No one in Wal gets paid without a license. And you know I won't take a license. You can't make me accept a lot in the life. No license and I take the jobs as I choose and the Storemaster don't like me getting paid there, especially since the thing with the Ditch Witch."

"I'm sure I have a quarter pound of bacon I could spare," I said.

"That's a lot of bacon," said Cooper, scratching his scalp with one hand and under his arm with the other. "Taxes on that, I'm sure. And I don't have a license. If you could pay me up front, pay me here instead of Wal, but I can't go in there just yet. No one in or out without a license or an invitation. Those that try are befucked if they do and becalmed if they don't."

"How come he can say the f-word?" asked Larry.

"Because he's an effing local," I said. "Now don't antagonize him. We're making a deal."

"Dude, he's totally shutting you down," said Larry.

"That's right," said Cooper. "I have to shut you down."

"I can get the bacon," I said.

"I can't go in there," said Cooper. "Not in there."

"Would this help?" said Larry. He held out a semi-circular object wrapped in grease-spattered yellow paper.

Cooper sniffed.

"It's a taco," said Larry. "Machaca. A little on the cold side, but still good."

Cooper came right up to Larry's hand and practically put his nose right on the taco.

"Yes," said Cooper. "Half now. Half when we get to the gate."

"And the deal is done, my brother," said Larry. He tore open the wrapper and broke the taco in half.

Cooper snatched the first half and devoured the cold greasy thing as though he hadn't eaten in days. Maybe he hadn't. This part of the future could be a hungry place, but not in Wal.

I grudgingly admitted that Larry had done well. A comment that he countered with a statement questioning if I had the intention of making a sexual advance. Fine, Larry. I won't say anything nice to you. Kicks to the groin from here on out.

COOPER HAD US QUICKLY on a deer path leading away from the main road and under the dark and creeping canopy of the woods proper. It was a bit of a hustle to keep up with the sprightly forest-urchin. Larry and I were both out of breath as we broke through to a meadow.

And, by meadow, I mean overgrown parking lot. If you knew what you were looking at, you could see the bent and rusted shafts of the abandoned light poles. A few trees broke through the sea of tall grass. A few scattered huts and outbuildings, as well as the hulk of an occasional SUV, punctuated the grassy plain that lead up to the walls of an ancient concrete warehouse-style big box store.

"And hence you've come to Wal," said Cooper.

"Here's your taco, bro," said Larry, handing Cooper the rest of it.

Without so much as a goodbye, Cooper grabbed his payment and ran for the woods.

And then, dammit all to hell, if Larry didn't lick his fingers and trigger his ludicrous taco-based time travel method on that tiniest, unmeasurable drip of grease. We jumped. Not very far. But we jumped.

We shifted straight into winter. In the blink of an eye a snow drift built up around us. We were still just a stone's throw away from Wal, but now we had to plunge through three feet of snow to get there.

Perhaps there had been an overcorrection to global climate change over the centuries. I'd never been to Wal in winter before. It was damn cold, and I wasn't dressed for it. Larry, with his Nordstrom poseur flannel and his canvas high-top sneakers, was going to die of exposure if we didn't get to shelter soon.

I considered pulling out my watch and scratching the mission. But this was one hell of a teachable moment. How would he learn from the natural consequences of accidentally time shifting if I bailed him out right away? Plus, I kind of like to see him suffer.

And the suffering was just beginning.

"Holy crap, these things are hot!" he yelled as he dropped the saw blades into the snow.

"Wait a minute," I said. "You carried the saw blades on that jump?"

He answered with an unceremonious "duh."

"That doesn't usually happen," I said.

"You carry all kinds of crap with you," said Larry.

"Inside my coat," I said. "The aura effect covers the exterior of your clothing and includes small personal items that have been steeped in your temporal footprint. But those saw blades... they really shouldn't have made the jump with you."

"Whatever," he said. "They're melting through this snow bank."

"Pick them up!"

"You pick them up!"

The diamond saw blades had melted their way deep into the snow. They'd be as good as gold in Wal. While I was sure I had some credit on the Storemaster's ledger, it was always better not to arrive empty-handed.

I sucked it up, and plunged my arms into the snow. The blades were still warm.

"Larry, I'm not sure what you are, but you are something different."

"Dude," he said, "I already told you it's a waste of time to hit on me like that."

"I ought to hit on you with my fist," I said. "Let's get to town before we start losing toes."

WE DIDN'T HAVE TO BLAZE much of a trail before we hit a cleared path. It was easy going to the first gate, vaguely recognizable as something cannibalized from the ruins of several shopping cart corrals.

"Holla, travelers," barked the guard at the gate. "What business have you at this, the darkest night of the darkest season of Wal?"

"Goods for sale," I said. "I know it's late, but I do have an account on the ledger. I'd like food and lodging for me and my assistant. We can do business in the morning."

The guard pulled his hat up out of his face and looked at us.

"Ishmael?" he asked.

"The one," I said.

"Get in here before the dogs show up." He opened the clumsy gate. "Hurry. It's an evil time. An evil time, but Hannie will set you up for the night."

"What kind of evil?"

"Best not to talk of it while the sun is leaving the sky," he said. "Let's just say there's a Burning on the morrow."

Ritual Burnings were not altogether unheard of, but they never happened in Wal. Brookland, maybe. And in the Meatlands, for sure. But never in Wal. The Storemasters had always looked upon Burnings as being bad for business. Things were definitely not right here.

"Would I know who's up for Burning?" I asked.

"I hate to say," said the guard, tying up the slats of the gate. "But it's that Cooper boy."

"Hey," said Larry, with a stupid grin, "I know that guy."

"Don't be so happy, Larry," I said. "They're planning on lighting him on fire tomorrow."

"What the hell?" he said. "I thought you said this place was chill?"

"It was," I said. "It's supposed to be. I've got to figure out what happened to my town."

"Oh," said the guard. "One more thing." He handed us each a small, clay jug. "Merry Christmas!"

At least there was some civility left in Wal, but a Christmas Burning? Things had gone seriously wrong.

Chapter 10
Goodnight Wal

(*Larry*)

Things got pretty screwed pretty fast. Oh, yeah, this is Larry's handwriting, in case you didn't figure it out. The little X's dotting the I's should be a dead giveaway, but this pen kind of sucks and they bleed into little turdy blobs.

Anyway, the first thing that happens when we get to Wal is that the dude at the gate gives us each a jug of beer. That was actually a good thing. And Ishmael was super on board with enjoying it right away, promising that there'd be plenty more. He pretty much downed his in a couple chugs. I'm not sure how Ishmael was able to stand after that, because that stuff was some serious malt liquor, but he was. Fair enough.

Ishmael led me through the town, which, let's get real here, looked like it was built out of a shopping center that used to be anchored by a K-Mart, or something. Classic mini-mall parking lot set up, only all the pavement was tore up and piled into a bitching rampart all around the place. It was kind of trippy to see it all turned inside out like that, but the jug of beer helped alleviate any disorientation I might have felt. It was pretty much just another Saturday night like I spent in high school, wandering through Cienega Village buzzing on stolen wine coolers. Let me tell, you, though, that shit in the brown jug was not wine coolers. Not by a long shot. That stuff knocked me on my ass before I knew it. They must have fortified it with moonshine or something because, dude, it was pretty all right.

Anyway, that bumpkin boilermaker had me feeling so good I didn't even notice at what point Ishmael was no longer my good drinking buddy. All I know is it was sometime after we had stumbled into Hannie's Hostel (Hannie's a really cool lady, by the way; I'll tell you about her later) and sometime before some local puke tried to steal those stupid saw blades I'd been carrying around.

Saw blades. Who knew they'd be such a hot commodity? Ishmael, I suppose. But that's his line of work.

So, I'm parked at a table in the dining room at Hannie's, totally enjoying the food and drink. It was some kind of stew with potatoes and, I'm guessing, rabbit. It went with the beer super good. So I'm putting a spoonful of the stew in my cakehole when I look down and see a grubby hand reaching out from under the table. At first I'm kind of on guard because I'm worried that the hand is looking for my junk. I'd heard about that sort of thing happening in highway rest stop bathrooms, so why not here, right?

But no. That hand was going straight for the blades I had sitting next to me ever since Ishmael told me to guard them with my life (Did he tell me that? He told me something. It's kind of a blur.)

What happened next is pretty much a testament to what kind of badass I can be if I'm buzzed out of my mind.

That spoon that was in my mouth? I brought that sucker straight down and embedded into the back of the thieving hand. Then I grabbed the arm and hauled this dirty, skeevy asshole out from under the table and had him up against the wall with my dinner knife at his throat.

I know, right? Where the hell did that come from?

I was waiting for the inevitable nugget of destructive criticism from Ishmael, so I could tell him to fuck off, but it never came. That's when I knew I was probably in for some shit.

Meanwhile...

(*Ishmael*)

I HATED TO LEAVE THE kid on his own like that, but I had something I needed to get to the bottom of. Namely, this question of Cooper being up for the Christmas Burning. Too many things were wrong with that situation.

It was easy enough to park Larry at Hannie's and head straight for the seat of authority in Wal: the Storemaster's Vault. The current Storemaster and I went way back. He was a hard man, a shrewd trader, and the kind of leader Machiavelli would have used as a case study if the two had ever had the privilege to meet. Not to imply he was an evil man, far from it. But the Storemaster of Wal knew exactly what the stakes were, how conniving and untrustworthy the other political forces in his world were, and that if he had any hope of keeping his family and his town safe he had to be ruthless toward the outside world.

But Cooper was one of his, if Cooper could be said to belong anywhere, it was Wal. Despite everything Cooper had said about refusing to take a license or a lot in Wal, which was an ongoing thing with him, the Storemaster, and Wal, still looked out for him far better than any of the other communities out there at the end of civilization. What could have happened that set the odd little man up to become a ritualized human sacrifice?

And what was up with that?

Every single one of the past nine Storemasters and I had an agreement about that. No killing as punishment, and no killing for holiday rituals. Up until now, I had assumed that agreement held with the current holder of the title.

Before heading off for a powwow with the Storemaster, I had a few words with the proprietor of the Hostel.

Hannie was my kind of post-apocalyptic woman. Tough as nails, stronger than dirt, and half a dozen other clichéd metaphors for exactly the kind of person you wanted to have on your side in a fight. She wasn't too bad to look at, either. About my age, but the crow's feet and gray hairs suited her. She had a habit of squinting which made me really wish I could cache a pair of bifocals for her, but I'm no optician. I'd undoubtedly get the prescription wrong. If it weren't for the fact that she was practically married to her job, I'd make a pass at her.

But who am I to ruin a good thing? Hannie and I go way back, just like everyone in Wal.

Here's a little secret. I know I make it a habit to be a cagey man, but I'll let this one out: Of all the places in human history, Wal's the one I come back to the most. It might not be the most profitable destination, but it's the destination that feels the most like home. I help them out when I can. And, for the record, just about every time I come to Wal, they could use some help.

"Hannie," I said. "What's this I hear about a Burning?"

"Ish," she said. "These are befouled times. There've been raiders on the freight trails. And the trade's not coming through like it should."

"There have been raiders before," I said. "The Storemasters have always been able to muster up a crew to deal with them."

"This time it's too much. Ghastly murders. People so rendered, strew, and fouled upon that the dogs won't even touch them."

"Fouled upon?" I asked.

"Fouled," said Hannie, confirming, but not clarifying. "Fouled, befouled and fouled upon." As much as I loved this town, the local idioms could be quite opaque at the best of times. At the worst of times clear communication was absolutely shittered.

"And why is Cooper going to the Burning Block?"

"Oh, Cooper," she said. "He's a boy-man who just can't stay in. You know he's back and forth between here and Brookland three times a week, running freight faster than the wagons."

"Yes, he's fast. And also useful. The dogs won't touch him."

"The dogs take him for one of their own," she said. "And maybe he is. Fact is he's the only one running freight without getting murdered. It's suspicious. A mob of folks engulfed and foreclosed upon him."

"That doesn't wash, Hannie. The Storemaster doesn't let the folks mob up for murder."

"Might have used to'n been true, but we've got a new Storemaster."

"Lizzabets?" I asked.

"No, but close," she said. "Stokes. The husband that come here from her all the way from the Cleaver."

"Right," I said. "It's nice to see that ten generations of trying to massage this place away from being a patriarchy is getting me nowhere."

"Weren't my doing," said Hannie. "Though I wouldn't know anything about how good a job Lizzabets would do. Never met her. Her father never let her out of the Vault."

"I'm getting to the bottom of this. Look after my apprentice."

(*Larry*)

Pretty freaking awesome, right? I had the dude against the wall like I was Schwarzeneggar. He was a scrawny guy. Probably just a kid, and I started feeling kind of bad that he had the spoon sticking out the back of his hand like that.

But he was trying to take my shit, and I was still pretty drunk. Things are bound to happen.

Hannie, was right there in the middle of it.

"All right, you two! Enough of that."

I dropped my knife, even as I realized the crappy blade on it wouldn't cut through anything that hadn't already been boiled into submission. Like, it was duller than the damn spoon I was eating with, right? In these situations, though, I suppose it's all about the attitude.

Hannie took the kid and looked at his hand. The spoon came out with a wince. She poked around and the kid cussed some words I wish

I could remember. I could use them on my asshole roommates in San Diego.

"You're lucky, Chippie," she said. "It missed your finger-strings."

The kid cussed some other stuff as Hannie poured some hot tea over his hand. It was probably some kind of herbal stuff, because I'd be very surprised if they had Earl Grey in stock.

"That should clean it out," she said. Then she wrapped his hand up with the most stained piece of cloth that ever got used for a bandage. I guess they don't have Clorox either. "Now fuck of with ya," she shouted at him.

Then she turned and looked at me with that kind of intense, pull anything and I'll kick your ass, look that for some reason causes the blood to rush to my crotch. I mean, she was kind of old like Ishmael, but, not bad, you know? And it had pretty much been a sausage fest between me and Ishmael ever since Lovejoy ran off to do whatever timecop stuff she had to do. All I'm saying is, sometimes when you haven't seen a woman in a while, any kind of attention feels like special attention.

But it was pretty much understood she could kick my ass, so I wasn't going to try anything. Just kind of appreciate the proximity and mind my manners. But, you know. When you're in your twenties and a long way from home…

"Stop looking at me like that, you drunken little pervert."

"um," I said.

"I'm not saying Chippie didn't have that coming," said Hannie, "but you'd best be careful who you stick a spoon into around here. It's evil times. This town's hospitality toward you could be shittered before you know it."

At this point, I pretty much puked on the table. And then I passed out in the corner. Anti-climactic, I know, but what can I say?

While I was sleeping it off, someone, I'm pretty sure it was Hannie, slipped the saw blades under my head for a pillow. That totally didn't help my headache.

(Ishmael)

The basic layout of the town of Wal, if you've spent any time in late 20th/early 21st century America, looks pretty much like the preserved ruins of any shopping center anchored by a big box retailer. Hannies Hostel occupied the free-standing restaurant pad where you'd find your basic T.G.I. Appletuesday's franchise. The building itself, however, was hardly recognizable. The roof had fallen in and been rebuilt several times over the centuries. The cinderblock walls had held in place, but the windows had long ago been filled in with mosaics of bottles and jars mortared in place with mud and straw. Nature, in revolt against the constraints of the parking lot, had asserted trees bushes and an accumulation of topsoil against the walls themselves. The building's former self was unrecognizable, and the food was a hell of a lot better.

I was quite proud of what the place had become.

Between Hannie's and the Big Box of Wal, where the Storekeeper ruled from his Vault, there was a ramshackle assortment of huts and rough hewn houses. Some were obviously salvaged from the hulks of long idle RVs. Others were of newer construction, built from the ungraceful masonry of salvaged concrete chunks.

I should have kept a better eye out as I crossed through the warren of narrow alleys and avenues. But it was cold, and I didn't have a proper hat. I was busy pulling at my coat collar, trying to get it to cover as much of my head as possible, when someone hit me from behind.

Don't you just hate it when you're plans for an evening are suddenly ruined because you're too busy being unconscious?

Of course you do. That was a rhetorical question.

So that's how we spent Christmas Eve. I was unconscious; Larry was unconscious. Snow and darkness covered the land.

Chapter 11
Headaches

ONE HEADACHE (*Ishmael*)

I woke up somewhere dark and quite the opposite of warm. My head did not appreciate the bashing it had gotten the last time I was aware of anything. It was time to start being aware again.

So, I became aware of the darkness, the chill, a general dampness, and a smell I really didn't like. It was the smell of a room that sometimes, but not quite often enough, has a chamber pot in it. And there was the sound of a groan. It might have come from myself. The throbbing in my head was making everything seem louder and closer than it possibly could be.

I tested my senses and groaned once on purpose. I knew that was me for certain.

Another groan answered. Not me this time. I was sure of it.

I looked to where it came from and found myself able to distinguish shapes and silhouettes and the distinctly feral form of the man I'd hoped to inquire about.

"Cooper?" I called out.

"Hey ho!," he said. "Call him Ishmael, for here he is, far from sea, far, far from the sea, and so close to the fire."

"I heard you were to be guest of honor at the Christmas Burning."

"I've heard that, too," said Cooper, his voice trailing.

"I've also heard," I said, "that the Storemasters of Wal have always forbidden the Burnings that other, less civilized towns indulge in."

"There's been murder, call-him-Ishmael. Murder. Foreclosure. Clusterfuckery. A usurper sits upon the Reckoning Chair in the Vault of Wal."

"Who would dare?" I said. "The Storemasters have run Wal well and justly ever since the Crash." A few sentences with Cooper and I couldn't help slip into the stilted vernacular customary to the time and place.

"Freight company man from beyond Hank Harbor," said Cooper. "A murderer and a strongman. The dogs, my dogs, they're my pack now, the dogs, running and barking and so loyal to themselves alone, and me now, because they made me one. I'm part dog now, I suppose. Perhaps I'm married to the bitch, now? I don't know. The dogs only tell me so much. And it's purely symbolic. Not a physical thing. Don't think that. That's not a thing I do. Saving myself for the human kind of wife. Too much information. She's a good companion, though. Good family. Don't think wrong things about her. But the dogs only tell me so much. But the dogs acted in the woods. They foreclosed upon the murderer, but there's still the strongman. Stokes, usurper, and his strongman, stepped in as the Storemaster choked on his pudding."

That Cooper. His tangled mind. What was he trying to tell me?

"You left, call-him-Ishmael!" said Cooper. "I brought you to Wal. I brought your 'prentice. I ate your taco. Then, shits! You left. Gone, bereft, alost. You were gone, even though I told you murder was coming to town."

"Settle down, Coop," I said. "It wasn't intentional. A glitch. My 'prentice dragged me into winter and here we are now."

"The Storemaster was not honestly choked," said Cooper. "I'm sure it was Stokes's fuckery that laid him low. And on a night you should have been here."

"I should have," I said. "My 'prentice is the root of some fuckery in his own right. I'm sorry."

"Sorry's not keeping Stokes from shoving a Christmas tree up my ass and lighting it."

"No," I said. "But maybe I can make something happen."

"Make it happen quick," said Cooper. "Christmas is coming."

The headache was making it hard to plan on the fly. I had to think of what allies I might be able to count on. There was Larry, I suppose, but after that taco grease incident, it was obvious he was still more of a liability than an asset. Hannie was always good in a fight, but she was also the kind who always kept her best interest first and foremost in mind. It had been years since I'd been in Wal, maybe a decade their time. I had very little idea what the micropolitics were like lately beyond what I could decode from Cooper's ravings. But, as a rule, the people of Wal knew how fairly they've always been treated. They tended to be very loyal to the hereditary line of Storekeepers. There could be someone to rally the townspeople. If only the headache would quiet down I could remember. Then, there it was, the memory I needed:

"Didn't the Storemaster have a daughter?" I asked.

"Indeed," said another voice. "I'm in here, too."

The Storemaster's daughter's voice. Young, bitter, with an underlying hint of pleasantness that would have show more strongly if the situation were not that of an ersatz dungeon. That is to say, she would have had a pretty voice if she wasn't locked in a room that smelled like a toilet.

"Well, shits," I said. "Back to the old dry erase board."

I had to think, but it was so hard. Probably concussed, which was bad because, in almost every case like this, it was by brainpower alone that I had any shot of survival. Brainpower, and the emergency default setting on my time machine.

Unconsciously, my hand dipped into the pocket where I kept my method, great-great grandpa's time traveling watch. Unconsciously, my hand found nothing there.

"Double shits."

ANOTHER HEADACHE (*Larry*)

I was thirsty. Oh, hell, was I thirsty. Cottonmouth didn't even begin to describe it. More like there was a whole sheep in there, and he was kicking at the inside of my skull just for the hell of it.

Plus, my pillow was totally bogus. Frickin' diamond saw blades. I know these things aren't worth whatever trouble I was in now, because... because... well, I couldn't come up with any specific reasons at the time, but I was pretty sure that, by that point, the whole deal was bullshit.

This, however, and I have to admit, is pretty much how I feel about mornings in general. Only this morning, I wasn't just hungover, I was hung at a steep incline with large, scavenger birds tapping at my skull and crapping down my shirt.

Plus, I had this stack of diamond saw blades leaving the impression of the chuck-hole on my face. I don't even know if chuck-hole's what it's called, but just imagine your flesh pressed through the hole in the middle of a circular saw blade and becoming a bright red super-zit that is surely not going to impress any of the local lady action, and you've got a good idea why I might be pissed about it.

The worst part, though, was someone was shaking me. Some son of a B was trying to wake my ass up. This was an especially harsh realm because the more awake I got, the more I felt it in my bones that I was sleeping on the cold hard floor of the pub I passed out in the night before.

"C'mon, slacker," said this voice that was like an older crustier version of someone I had met before. I couldn't quite place it, though, what with all of holy hell ringing through my skull.

"It's time to get your pissant self up off the pavement," he said.

"erunnnh," was about all I could manage as I peeled my face off the saw blades and turned my bleary head in his direction.

"Here," he said. "Drink this."

Something was up against my face, something hot that smelled kind of like flowers and dirt.

"What is this?"

"It's what passes for coffee around here," he said.

"It'll have to do, I guess."

I took a drink and hell if that shit didn't open my eyes. I finally could get a look at the dude who woke me up.

He was an older guy, but a tough older guy. One of those codgers you wouldn't want to mess with. Like equal parts Frank Sinatra and hobo king. I know that's kind of a contradiction, but you'd know what I mean if you saw this guy's blue eyes plus his thrift store bargain bin outfit. His trench coat itself looked like it might have spent all of World War I in an actual trench. Everything else was tatters, patches, and grease stains, but, somehow, in a way that set his clothes apart from the sack cloth and furs attire of the locals.

"All right, sunshine," said the guy. "We've got to get moving if we're going to save our friend Ishmael from the fire."

"Hold on," I said. "You're obviously not from around here. You're also obviously not a time cop. Who the eff are you?"

The codger laughed. "Ishmael's been on your ass to clean up your language, hasn't he?"

"Sure," I said, "but who the eff are you?"

"I'm the guy with the watch," he said.

Lo and behold, he had the thing right there, dangling by a braided leather fob: Ishmael's mother trucking time travel watch. Who the eff was this guy?

Chapter 12
Queequeg

(*Larry*)

"Wait a minute wait a minute wait a goddamn minute," I said. "How'd you get Ishmael's watch."

"It's my damn watch," the old dude said. He pulled out one of those little notebooks that English majors like and flipped through it quickly. "Give me a minute, here. I did my homework earlier, but it never hurts to check your notes. Let's see. You sure as hell aren't Lovejoy, so you've got to be Larry."

"Yeah," I said. "But who are you? And why do you have my bro's watch?"

"Bro?" he said. "Oh, I don't believe you two are related."

"No, man, he's not my brother. That's, like, a figure of speech. But he is my, I don't know the word for it. Boss, I guess. But I'm not getting paid. So, what do you call that, and why do you have his watch?"

"Like I said before," said the old guy, blue eyes ready to drill holes in my face, "it's my watch. Ishmael's only borrowing it."

"Oh..." it clicked. You know how it feels when something clicks? Kind of like getting some unexpected overtime hours on that paycheck for the job you hate. "You're Ishmael's grandpa!"

"Great-great grandfather, to be precise."

"Whatever, gramps," I said.

Then he slapped me upside my head.

"Don't call me 'gramps,'" he said. "If you've got to call me anything, call me Queequeg."

"Queequeg?" I said. "What the hell kind of name is Queequeg?"

"A literary one," he said. "If *he* can be Ishmael, I can be Queequeg."

"Sure, whatever," I said. "I was just totally expecting Ahab."

"'Whatever,' indeed," said Gramps. "Grab those saw blades. We've got a jailbreak to engineer."

SO, WE HAD SOME EQUIPMENT to gather. Apparently Gramps had connections in that town. At least one, at any rate. He hollered over at Hannie about some crate he had stashed in her shed. She threw a ladle at him and said not to shout so early in the morning. I tell you what, the sexual tension was *not* rife between those two. They were more like inlaws. I suppose Gramps was too old, anyway. Cause, like I said, Hannie still definitely had it. Gramps on the other hand, well, let's just say the moniker Queequeg does not detract from his charms.

Anyway, after Hannie chased us out of her establishment we had to shuffle through some hip-deep snow out to what was probably once one of those sheet metal sheds my uncle filled his backyard with. It was hard to say, though, because the thing had been braced, reinforced, rebuilt and repainted about fifty times in three centuries. It could have started out as a double-wide manufactured home for all I knew. At least it looked like it might have been one of my uncle's tool sheds. Some parts, where the metal paneling showed through all the reinforcing crap, the paint on it was so thick it looked like butter cream frosting. I wouldn't eat it, though. I wouldn't be surprised if humanity had cheaped out and went back to lead-based paint at some point between my time and now.

So, Grampy Queequeg goes into the shed and bangs around looking for whatever. Show and icicles are shaking off the roof, and I swear the whole thing's liable to fall in on him at any minute. And he's bitching up a storm.

"Of course the effing thing has to be underneath every other damn piece of crap tool and gewgaw Ishmael's dragged here over the years," he says.

Then he calls for me to get my ass in there, so I'm like, okay, I'm three hundred years in the future and I'm going to die in a tin shed catastrophe.

So, in this little eight by ten deathtrap, there's this bad-ass looking, old fashioned style wooden crate buried under lawn mowers and extension cords and a gasoline powered generator and a bunch of other stuff.

"Why all this?" Gramps bitched. "Did Ishmael seriously think he would be able to get a hold of any gas to run this? Get it off my crate for me."

"Where should I put it?"

"I could give a shit," he said. "Out in the snow, if you have to." I kind of liked Gramps' attitude.

"I told you not to call me 'Gramps.'"

Have I been narrating out loud?

Anyway, it took a few minutes of careless, random hucking of stuff, but we got everything cleared off of the trunk. Grampy Queequeg handed me a pry bar and I popped off the lid.

Inside the crate was a pair of Igloo coolers like what you'd fill with the beers you were taking to your buddy's pool party. Gramps popped open one of them and shuffled through what looked like a bunch of papers. He pulled out at big poster-sized architectural drawing looking thing. "Hope the utility connections are accurate on this."

Then he closed that cooler up tight and opened the other one. Out of that, I'll be damned if he didn't pull a corded circular saw.

"Looks like we'll need that generator after all," I said.

"Nuts to that," he said. "I've got an extra-universal adaptor."

NEXT THING I KNOW IS Gramps is having me lug this industrial grade circular saw and the stupid saw blades across the damned snow again. I realized then that, if I was going to keep up this time travel business, I was going to have to trade my canvas Chucks for something more water resistant. I'd always thought Doc Martin's were too punk for the kind of loving vibe I wanted my fashion choices to send out, but I was starting to worry about losing toes. Besides, the 'loving vibe' hasn't been working for crap anyway. I'm getting zero action with it.

So, Gramps was following these yellowed architectural plans like they were a pirate's treasure map. We were carefully counting our paces and checking our positions against landmarks, like how many rusted out lamp posts we tripped over. And the sun wasn't even up yet.

"I've got to hand it to you, Grampy Queequeg," I said. "You sure know how to show a guy a good time on his birthday."

"Bullshit," he said. "You don't have a birthday within 250 years of now." He was right. It really wasn't my birthday. I'm not even sure why I said that. Sometimes I just say things, because I feel things need to be said. Just because. You know what I'm saying? But, actually Gramps was still talking, so I'll get back to what he was saying. In full on crotchety grandpa mode, he was all, "quit your bellyaching. We've got to spring Ishmael from jail, or I'm never going to get my watch back."

"But I thought you have your watch now," I said.

"Technically, yes, I do," he said. "But, it's complicated. There's a thing with a thing, and a gambling debt, and a talking allosaurus."

"A talking allosaurus like Jorge-George?" I said, remembering the freaky incident in my old neighborhood where the taco truck turned out to be smuggling dinosaur meat.

"So you've met Horkachorge?" he said. "Yeah, well, you can appreciate that, like any dealing with a talking dinosaur, things are convoluted as all hell. But the long and short of it is, if Ishmael ends up being the guest of honor at the Christmas bonfire, my ass is grass. Plus, I'm only holding onto the watch now, because Ishmael and I are both here at the same time and the watch can only exist once at the same time, and since it's mine, it's with me."

I had no idea what that all meant, but I could tell it was my turn in the conversation to say something. I took a stab at it.

"So, Ishmael doesn't have his watch?"

"What did I just say?" said Gramps.

"Honestly, I'm not sure, but I think we're busting Ishmael out of the pokey and that's all I really need to know."

"Fair enough," said Gramps.

We stopped at a place where the snow seemed to have fallen in on itself. It was sunken in, or something. I'm not sure how to describe it. Just, it was a spot where the snow seemed less.

"Did you bring a shovel?" he asked.

"Dude, I brought this freaking heavy-ass saw. What are you talking about?"

"Right," he said. "Set all that crap down a minute and take this shovel."

He threw the shovel at me like it was a spear. I caught it, but crap, Grampy Queequeg was one of those world class dangerous old guys. You gotta watch out for him. Who knew he'd have a shovel? Of course, it makes sense, him and Ishmael being related, the two guys in all of space and time who would have collapsible shovels tucked into their trench coats.

Luckily, all I really had to do with the shovel was clear out the sunken in bit of snow from the opening of an old parking lot storm drain. The metal grate that would have covered it in a normal, from my time, parking lot had rusted away long ago. Once the snow was out of the way it was an easy shimmy into the tunnel underneath.

The tunnel was pretty good size. I could almost, almost stand up in it. I had to crouch a little bit, but no big deal. The tunnel was dark as all hell, though.

Of course, Gramps had a solution for that as well. He fired up this crazy ass tiki torch that, whatever it was burning, smelled a lot more like barbecue than citronella. Recycled cooking grease, I'm sure. It would have been a welcome smell if it weren't for the fact that this storm drain had some serious sewage odors going on in it.

Gramps was following the plans again and led us through a few zigs and zags, but nothing too tricky. Soon he picked out a spot on the wall.

"This'll be it," he said. He then grabbed a piece of charcoal from somewhere, his pocket, I guess. With the charcoal, he drew a square about two foot by two foot.

"All right, kid. If I'm reading my plans right, the basement they like to keep the houseguests in is on the other side of this wall. All we've got to do is cut along the dotted lines, and spring Ishmael."

I loaded up a saw blade, and pulled my shades out of my pocket for eye protection. Safety first, right? But there was something that seemed like a pretty big deal, a nigh insurmountable problem.

"Where are we going to plug this thing in?" I said.

"That's what I brought the extra-universal adaptor for," he said. "We're going to run it off the watch. It'll be slicker than shit. You'll see."

So, he laid out this weird, extension cord thing in front of him. He plugged the watch in on one end of the cord and the circular saw on the other. I was pretty sure it wasn't going to work because, a watch, right? Who runs a saw off a watch battery?

But the saw fired up like a champ. In fact, I was this close to losing my foot because I wasn't expecting it to turn on at all. I just about dropped it as it came to life. So much for safety first.

Anyway, that saw was actually a bit small for the job, but what are you going to do? Take it back to Home Depot with a 300 year old receipt? Not really. I started working on cutting the wall and Gramps would splash some god-awful sewer water on the blade every now and then. It made the cutting a little easier, but everything sure stank to high hell.

Even with the wetting, the first blade crapped out before I was done with the first cut. We had two more blades, but, at this rate we'd blow through them before completing our escape hole.

"I suppose it was too much to expect this to go smoothly," said Gramps. Then he took his charcoal and drew a diagonal slash through his square outline. "Let's make it a triangle. And try to at least score all the edges before going for broke and cutting through. We may have to take a sledge and bust it out the old fashioned way."

"You're the boss," I said. "One more thing, though."

"Yeah?"

"What's that sound?"

At first I had thought it was just the sound of my teeth settling back into their sockets after the vibrations of the saw. But that didn't really make sense, because I'm a person, not a cartoon.

It was a skittering sound. One of those menacing, skittering sounds, like what you hear when the rats have come to finish your roommate's KFC that he left in the middle of the living room before passing out last night. Only this was a bigger menacing skittering than I was used to.

Grampy Queequeg waved his torch around, hoping to catch whatever it was in its light.

And there it was. For a second, I thought it was one of those freaky hairless cats, but it didn't have ears, and it wasn't really standing like a cat, and it was totally the wrong shape, and its skin looked more like iguana skin than the saggy old lady at the pool skin those cats kind have.

"Crap," said Gramps. "Velociraptors."

Chapter 13
Darkness and Exposition

(*Ishmael*)

"Wait a minute! Wait a goddamn minute," I said. "How did somebody snatch my watch?"

This was unprecedented. The watch had never left me before. It had never been further away than a quick dip into my pocket, and it had never been taken from me despite some of the more unfriendly pat down searches I've been subjected to. Basically anytime I'd go to the airport, or get stopped at the border, or wind up in the middle of a home invasion gone south, the watch always slipped itself into a fold of clothing opposite the direction of the searching hands. And it always found its way to a ready pocket just when I needed it. I don't like getting mystical, but the thing was fucking made of magic like that. And, as such, it always seemed to be charmed against theft and loss, at least until now.

Now.

'Now.' There's a word that quickly loses its meaning when I start writing about my adventures. Is it 'now,' as in the immediate right effing now of right now? Or is it the 'now' of some distant time a couple hundred years after anyone who would ever care to read this, and be able to read this, are dead and gone? Or is it the 'now' of the relatively recent past, at least in a strictly literary sense, the relatively recently written down? 'Now' was here; 'now' was then. When the hell is this 'now' I'm talking about? 'Right now,' which either means immediately, or whenever I get around to it? Now. Now now. Right now. (Did I mention the headache I was getting over?)

Now, before I get too far along in this passage, I want to apologize for a grievous violation of the storyteller's art. This week's episode is light on action and heavy on talkie-talkie backstory revealing. Otherwise known as a snooze fest. I can't help it, though. I was pretty much locked in a dark room with a batshit back country courier and the daughter of the most powerful man in Wal. It was pretty much like the set up of a bad joke, or a Sartre play, only instead of being in a farmhouse, or in Hell, we were in a stuffy, unlit room where one of the corners had been dedicated to use as a toilet.

Sartre said hell was other people. I'd like to supply a corollary: hell can also be inadequate sanitation.

That corner... it hadn't been used as a toilet for long. But recently, and the room was damp. And that was enough, and without my watch, I was growing desperate. Between the miasmic fug in the room, and my lingering headache, some horrible ideas for plans of action were leaking into my mind. I was actually contemplating searching that godforsaken corner for my watch when Cooper chimed in on my train of thought.

"Watch the watch," he said. "We've all lost what we've been watching. I mean, I'm mean? Mean the mean the mean... the watch where you're going! Did you do that? Did you watch? Watch your watch? Would we be here if you had? I told you, Ishmael, there was *murder*, and where were you?"

He had told me something about murder, but at the time, and now as well, I couldn't figure out how any of the rest of the words in his sentences related to anything in the real world. They did relate to something, I'm sure. I trusted that there was some sort of message buried in his urgency, but Cooper was far more accustomed to talking to himself than to other people. Besides, I could tell trying to understand him through the smell and headache was only going to get on my nerves.

I turned to the other occupant of our ersatz dungeon, the daughter of the Storemaster. I'd never talked to her before, only seen her in the background as I dealt with her father on occasion. Her father, until very lately, and now just late, the Storemaster of Wal, was one of the cagiest sons of bitches there ever was. His cageyness suited his position, but I never felt like I'd made a real connection with him, not the way I had with the other Storemasters. I wasn't quite sure how to proceed with his daughter, so, for expedience's sake, I settled on straight up blunt.

"Tell me, princess," I said. "What's going on here?"

"Why do you care, Ishmael the Outsider?" she said. "You only come when things are slack, you play a bit, eat and drink, then skip away. Now you're here when we're betroubled. What to do? Just skip away, like you always do."

Apparently it was an 'everyone hates Ishmael' kind of day. If my watch hadn't gone AWOL, I would have been sore pressed not to just 'skip away.' But I was stuck, so I had no recourse other than stick up for myself, and hopefully figure out what was really in store for us.

"Listen, princess," I said, "I've been here for plenty of hard times, *you* just don't remember them."

"It's true," said Cooper. "His stink was all over these woods twelve winters ago when Wal almost starved, and Brookland *did* starve."

That must have been when I busted up a ring of highwaymen that were interfering with the overland trade from Hank Harbor. An early storm hit and their animals froze. They had five sledges worth of corn and beans and horded and no way to get it anywhere to sell it. They were almost thankful when I showed up ahead of the posse from Wal. I don't like killing. The option I gave them was something just short of that, a head start, but it was a better deal than what they would have got from the others.

"I was a child," she said. "But is this man old enough to have been a man when I was a child?"

I took that as a testament to the diligence I paid to dental hygiene. Nothing ages you like a mouth full of blackened nubs where your teeth used to be. Try as I might, I never could convince the people of Wal that flossing paid off in the long run.

"I age differently than most, princess."

"I wish you wouldn't call me princess," she said. "I never was a princess. This is no kingdom."

Cooper snorted. And snorted again. Then it seemed like he was scratching at the floor. Evidently it had nothing to do with our conversation. It was just creepy. I liked Cooper, but I liked him better in a well lit room.

"I apologize," I said. "What should I call you?"

"My name," she said.

"Which is?"

"That's right," she said. "You're too busy to figure out what anyone's name is." Say what you will about civilization going downhill, here at the bottom end of it, young women could be just as sanctimonious as anyone you'll find in the Modern Era.

"I'm sorry if your father never bothered to introduce us," I said. "Ours was strictly a professional relationship. He made that clear, for sure. He became Storemaster quite young, and kept everyone at arm's length. Especially me. The Storemasters before him remembered me and invited me to all the feasts, introduced me to all their children, thanked me for helping keep this tiny pocket of humanity safe and strong when the Crash hit and ever since. But your dad never trusted anyone he didn't feel certain he could kill with his bare hands. He was cagier than anyone I ever knew, and I respected that. But we were never close. And he never brought me home for dinner. So, what am I going to do? Introduce myself?"

"You could start with that," she said.

"I could," I said, "but I'm an ornery cuss and it's going to take a minute to swallow my pride." And this was true. I am an ornery cuss. "I'm sorry we couldn't have met under better circumstances. I'm Ishmael. That Ishmael. The one the old folks talk about. To whom do I owe the pleasure?"

"Lizzabits," she said. "My name's Lizzabits, but my father called me Bits. That's probably how he'd have introduced me, although I would hate to hear anyone use his pet name for me after what happened to him."

"So, what happened?"

"Father got ill a few months ago," she said.

"Murder..." Cooper snorted.

"A silver tongued usurper asshole befriended his way into the Vault," Lizzabits continued. "He brought a girl from Brookland and said she was me. No one noticed, because you're not the only one father never introduced me to."

"I noticed," said Cooper. "And I told you, Ishmael. I told you 'murder.'"

"And I was on my way, Coop. Something annoyingly unforeseen delayed me."

"You should have been here earlier," said Cooper. "I had you here. But a strange, broken wind came and you rode it to winter."

"Something like that," I said. It was Larry and his damned taco grease. The simple act of licking his fingers had buggered us out of what would have been a much smoother insertion point into the chain of local events. What would happen now if he ate some Mexican food while I was separated from my watch? Would I still travel with him? Or had the Orb merely linked our methods and not our persons? Without my method in hand, was I destined to end my days in Wal? Boy, was great-great gramps going to be pissed if I couldn't get the watch back to him. How was that going to work, anyway?

Anyway... anyway...

Anyway, I was in Wal, and if I had to be marooned in my own future, Wal was as good a time and place as any, so long as I could sort out this usurper business before my cellmates and I all got burned at the stake for Christmas.

"Let me connect some dots," I said. "This usurper helped your father run the affairs of Wal. Stayed close. Handled all the communications. Perhaps even helped the Storemaster's illness dig in a little deeper. Then, when your father was delirious and just about to death's door, the usurper dressed up his Brookland girl as you and invited the town to a little wedding."

"More or less," said Lizzabits. "First he proposed marriage to me directly, but I refused. That's when his Brookland whore arrived and I was shoved in this forget-me-hole. Soon after the trothing feast, the usurper came down here himself to tell me father had passed and that, because I had no brother, he was now the Storekeeper."

"That's bullshit," I said. "I had a hand in writing the *Codes and Lots in the Life of Wal.* Nothing in there says anything about the Storekeeper's Lot falling to a male heir. Or any heir. It's set up as—"

"Everyone in this room knows this is bullshit," said Cooper. "Even those of us who don't have a bullshit Lot in the Life of Wal to begin with. I am who I am and everyone knows it and that's why the Christmas burnings are on." As Cooper said this, I could hear the agitated scraping of his feet along the floor, as though he were spinning in circles or something. He really was not the kind of guy who could stand being locked inside for any length of time.

"That's the other thing our usurper promised," said Lizzabits. "A 'return to the traditions of the land.' Traditions like the burnings."

"More bullshit," I said.

"Perhaps," said Lizzabitsits, "but so long as the town keeps eating it, the usurper will keep shoveling it."

"Does this usurper have a name?" I asked.

"Stokes," said Cooper. "Stokes the fire. Stokes the burning. He has three of us. Three candles in the park. Oh, what a Hell of some things that will be."

I don't know if it was the content or the context, but Cooper's words had never seemed clearer to me, which was frightening enough in itself.

"We've got one thing going for us, though," said Cooper.

"What's that?"

"The dogs hate him. Oh, do the dogs *hate* him! Wait until spring, Stokes. Spring is coming, Stokes! *Spring is coming!*"

At that, Cooper began to wail, a high, keening wail. There were no words, just sound. The only light came from the cracks around the door, and that was faint. Nothing distinct could be seen, but the fluttering of limbs. Cooper was not doing well.

And then I heard something else, a sound akin to Cooper's keening, but more mechanical in nature. Nothing was certain, but it sounded like the whine of a 300 year old circular saw blade destroying itself against 300 year old concrete.

Larry? Could the little twerp actually be up to something productive on his own?

Chapter 14
Crap, Velociraptors

(*Larry*)

I almost dropped the saw on my foot.

"Did you say 'velociraptors'?" I asked. I mean, gramps was old. Maybe he said that funny word for bicycle, and I misheard. He could have totally said bicycles. *Crap, bicycles,* is a thing that would totally make sense for someone to say in a dark storm drain sometime after the zombie apocalypse.

Okay, I wasn't sure it was a zombie apocalypse, but some apocalypse had happened. And we were in a small fortress town that had established itself in the bones of an old Target store, or something like that. But, who knows, I always sucked at history, so I'm not ruling zombies out. Velociraptors, on the other hand. I really wanted to rule them out.

"You bet your ass," said Queequeg. "Velociraptors."

Crap, velociraptors.

"So, we should hold totally still, right?" I asked. "And maybe they won't see us? Because they've got that dinosaur vision thing where they can only see movement."

Grampy Queequeg started laughing. It was one of those intense old guy laughs that progresses into a coughing fit and, sometimes, a really impressive loogie. Only Gramps just let it go as far as the first cough, then pulled he it together.

"What year is it for you?" he said. "Whenever it is you come from."

"Ninety-four," I said.

"Nineteen ninety-four. I should have guessed." As he was talking, Queequeg was unplugging the watch and the saw, and rolling up his crazy ass extension cord. "How many times did you see *Jurassic Park*?"

"About six," I said, "but most of those times I snuck in."

"Good for you," said Gramps. "That whole movie is full of shit. Look."

Queequeg, Gramps, whatever this dude's name really was, handed me his tiki torch. Then he reached in his coat and pulled out one of those big-ass flashlights cops like to beat on people with. He popped the switch and flooded the tunnel with the beam.

There were three of those creepy, hairless cat looking things. A little bigger than cats. They actually kind of looked like turkeys they way they were standing. They even kind of had feathers. Only they were skinny, feral turkeys. Not the Thanksgiving kind. They froze in the beam of the flashlight for a second, then tore off into the shadows further down the tunnel.

"So, where are the velociraptors?" I asked.

"That was them," said Queequeg.

"Really?" No effing way were those velociraptors. "They were, like, babies, right?"

"Full grown adults, kid," he said. "Spielberg's been steering you wrong. These little buggers only get so big. Scavengers mostly, so they aren't really a danger to something our size, unless we're sick or injured. Otherwise, you can just huck a rock at them, and they'll go chase after something easier to eat."

This was huge freaking relief, because I was expecting those six-foot sharks with legs from the movie.

"So, we're good, right?" I asked.

"Yes and no," he said. "The velociraptors themselves aren't so much of a problem. It's the larger predators they tend to follow around."

"So?"

"So," he said, "there's a larger predator around. Time to drop the saw, and let's run like hell."

He didn't have to tell me twice, because, I really had seen *Jurassic Park* six times. Not that it was that amazing of a movie, but because my buddy, Jared, worked at a movie theater and he'd sneak me in all the time. Mostly I'd show up because there was a girl working in the concession stand who I was trying to get to butter my popcorn, if you catch my meaning. But it turned out she's a lesbian, so, whatever, I stayed for the movie. I thought I learned a lot about dinosaurs.

Back in the post-apocalyptic storm sewer, it was a balls out foot race. It was like the both of us, Gramps and me, were trying to outrun his flashlight beam. Only, it turns out that's something that only happens in cartoons. I was thinking it might be worth a shot, because, hey, I'm a time traveler now. That's supposed to be impossible, so why not try some other impossible things?

Pshaw, right. I'm yanking your trousers. I knew we couldn't outrun the flashlight beam.

But we were running fast, and I was pretty surprised at how spry Gramps was. In fact, he tripped me at least twice when I tried to shove past him. I'm not sure what I landed in when I splashed down in the middle of the tunnel floor, but, actually, I have a good idea. I just don't want to admit it. We were pretty much in a sewer, right?

Twice that happened. Mark my words, Queequeg's got it coming. One way or another gramps is going to pay for his unsportsmanlike contact. Most likely I'll sharpie on his face when he's asleep.

Anyway, as we were running, I was trying to listen for the predator. Every time I could tune my ears to something beyond the sound of my own breathing and pounding heart, I strained for the 'thoom, thoom, thoom,' of some T-rexy, bite you in half, mother trucking dinosaur.

But all I heard was giggling. Giggling. Little kid giggling. Like someone told a fart joke to a kindergarten class. That didn't seem like it could be right, so I just kept running, trying to put as much of that tunnel between me and the predator as I could.

So, with some twists and turns, and a few elbows to the gut (old guys have some seriously sharp elbows), we burst back out into the morning daylight. It was still cold as hell outside, but I'd worked up a sweat. And there was all of god knows what running down my front from when I fell in the tunnel.

I took the opportunity for a victory flop onto the closest adjacent snow drift. The victory flop was short lived, however. There was a love tap to my ribs from Gramps' boot.

"What the hell are you doing lying on the ground, asshole?" he shouted.

"I thought we were done," I said as Gramps grabbed my arm and yanked me upright.

"We have to get back to—"

"Back to where?"

Gramps was cut off by a voice that sounded a little like a freight train testing the air brakes.

"Back to my banker," said Gramps, smiling. "So I can make a hefty withdrawal and settle up with your boss."

"Liar," said the voice. "Liar, liar, liar. That's all right, though. I rather enjoy the taste of liars."

In the background, the kindergarten giggles kicked in like crazy. I still hadn't looked up, because I really didn't want to see what I was afraid I would see. Plus, I had a bunch of snow in my eyes. Also, and this is kind of personal, I really didn't want to have sewage coating the inside, as well as the outside, of my pants.

"You can't eat me," said Gramps, to the... the whatever it was I didn't want to look at. "Aside from being so full of gristle I'm undigestible, I've got a privileged timeline."

"A privileged timeline?" said the voice, with hint of that special timbre sounding the way applying the brakes on a locomotive that can sound when used to convey the subtle tone of incredulity. (I totally stole that description. I'm not even sure what some of those words mean, but I got stuck when I was writing this part and asked for help.)

The giggling kindergartners piped up again.

I had to look.

It was somehow scarier than anything I could have imagined lying face down in that snow hill. First of all, as my eyes crept over toward the larger predator that I knew had to be there, I saw four turkey-sized velociraptors laughing their asses off. I will never be able to hear little kids laugh again without thinking of these creepy little bastards. They were rolling around and kicking their creepy claw feet in the air. And now I could definitely see they had feathers. Weird. Weird, ugly, creepy little tiny dinosaurs.

But, above them, the bigger dinosaur, the predator, the one that wanted to bite Queequeg in half, was standing there, like a super-sized version of the ugly turkeys, only he was wearing a red and white striped sweater and mirrored aviator glasses. I mean, what the fuck?!

"Yes," said Queequeg. "A privileged goddamn timeline. I didn't ask for it, it just happened, no matter how many people at CTCAHQ it pisses off."

The sweatered dinosaur started laughing. I hate it when dinosaurs laugh. This one sounded like everything you don't want to hear at the dentist's office. High pitched whines, the cracking of bone, and the receptionist telling you how much of it your dental plan isn't going to cover. Add to that the sound of the giggling little turkey bastards joining in.

And at that point, screw it, there's no prettying this one up, I shit my pants.

Chapter 15
Jailbroken

(*Ishmael*)

I should have known better than to get my hopes up. The splintering whine reverberating through our makeshift cell wall petered out long before any noticeable hole appeared. On the up side, Cooper had stopped his feral whine and was now quietly panting, or some such.

It was still dark. I couldn't tell what he was doing. He was just quiet, and that was a welcome change.

"It seems our rescuers have given up," said Lizzabits.

"I wouldn't abandon all hope yet," I said.

"So you have confidence in your apprentice?" she asked.

I had to think. I really hadn't been able to think for the half hour or so that the sawing sound, and Cooper's keening accompaniment, dominated everything but the smell in our dungeon. But now I could think and, hopefully, puzzle some pieces together. There had to be something more to Larry if he could figure out how to start up a power tool in this post-technological era beyond the total collapse of the North American power grid. Or it could just be dumb luck. Even if it was just dumb luck, the kid had a disproportionate allotment of it. It didn't seem absolutely outside the realm of possibility that he could work something out.

But I also had to be honest.

"I'm really not sure about Larry at all," I said. "He's pretty much a total fuck-up. But he's so unpredictable about it that I can't write us off just yet."

Lizzabits was quiet.

I was quiet.

Cooper panted softly in the corner.

"How many days till Christmas?" I asked.

"I've lost count of the days," said Lizzabits. "I haven't seen the sun since the usurper asshole threw me in here. All I know is that I was alone for quite a while. Then Cooper came. And then you, not long after."

"Any ideas, Coop?"

"The dogs are not happy," he said. "Their hunt's been spoiled."

"Okeydoke, captain non sequitur," I said.

I just don't know how to follow that crap up sometimes. But, if Cooper knew anything about anything, it would be the dogs. I just couldn't see how that would help the situation. In any case, he was still panting from the fit he threw over the whining, grinding sound from the other side of the wall.

We all sulked in silence for longer than is comfortable to relate.

Then, with no warning or preamble, the door banged open.

"Hurry up, please," said a burly man in the doorway. "It's time."

"Time!" shouted Cooper. "You don't know anything about time." This was followed closely by Cooper emitting a banshee wail and performing a savage feat of self-projection.

Cooper had the big man's face planted in the filth that lined the floor before anyone knew what was happening. It could hardly have been a planned attack, more like the sudden release of an over-tensed, twisted strip of metal. The guy needed out, and anyone between him and the direction of out was going to get hurt.

Myself, never having been one to shirk at an opportunity, I grabbed it.

"You coming, Liz?" I called as I peered out at the three stunned heavies lying on the floor in the corridor. Cooper was already long gone.

Lizzabits and I ran off down the hallway like poor imitations of the madman who had preceded us. The path was clear all the way to the stairs and up a flight. Things were looking very good. And the air was a lot clearer.

Alas, things just can't stay good for me for long, sometimes.

At the top of the stairs reinforcements had arrived.

They were four more wads of muscle that were unfamiliar to me. I knew by sight pretty much everybody who had ever lived in Wal, so these were obviously outsiders Stokes had brought in.

"All right, you three," began one of them.

"There's only two," said another.

"Two?" said the first. "That's not right. We've got three Christmas trees set up." He gestured out too three trimmed evergreens set above tarped off mounds of what must be the kindling for the horrid affair they were planning. "Who ever heard of a Christmas Burning with only two?"

"Methinks," interjected one of the other guards, "that's the third one scaling the wall over there."

Indeed, Cooper had made it all the way across the courtyard and three quarters of the way up the rough, cyclopean masonry of the chunks of reclaimed concrete that formed the outer wall. In another breath he was gone.

"Well, that's befuggered it all," said the first. "We'll have to find another volunteer."

"Maybe," I said, "you could just call the whole thing off. Christmas Burning's not really a tradition in Wal, anyway."

"Not a tradition?" said the second tough. "How can you have a proper Christmas tree if you don't have someone tied to it when the kindling's lit."

"We just don't do that here," I said.

"And who are you that knows what 'we' do anyways?" said the first.

"He's Ishmael Fugit," said Lizzabits. "His family have been frequent advisors to all the Storemasters since the Crash. If anyone knows our traditions, it's him."

"Seems like he could have given the previous Storemaster some better advice," said the lead heavy. Then he started laughing. The others joined the laugh, including the ones coming up behind us, the downed heavies who were now recovering from Cooper's berserker escape rampage.

My hand instinctively reached for the watch that wasn't there. Where the hell was that thing? Not that I'd bail on young Lizzabits, but it would just be a bit more comforting if I knew I had the option of an emergency default handy.

"Right," said the leader of the heavies. "Gord, Lew. Help me get these two tied up. The rest of yis go find another volunteer. Maybe that wormy kid at the hostel."

What I wouldn't have given for a scary, pointy, truck-stop display case weapon of questionable efficacy right then. Or even an off-brand pry-bar. Anything solid and menacing to counteract the solid and menacing barbarian futuroids that wanted to tie me to a tree and set me on fire.

Alas, my pockets had been turned out and emptied before I'd been thrown into that dungeon hole. They must have gotten the watch then, even though I couldn't believe a thug could snatch the miracle device off of me so easily. And now that I was without it, I had an eerie recollection of something great-great grandpa said. As he gave it to me, he said the watch treated us to a 'privileged timeline.'

He wouldn't go into specifics other than that there were a couple fixed points in the entire span of the history of the universe that depended on that watch being there. One was happening as he was giving me the watch. Another would come when I gave him the watch. Everything else, no matter how hairy or hellacious, would turn out all right because the watch knew where it needed to get, and we were along for the ride.

I kind of took it as bullshit at the time, but that watch had saved me from countless scrapes since then. I had come to believe in this 'privileged timeline' idea. But did that privilege hold up if I was separated from the watch?

Gord (I assume) was busy measuring out some length of a plastic rope woven from centuries old shopping bags, while Lew held me in place.

The captain of this crew of outside muscle had Lizzabits all to himself.

"Now you look sufficiently filthy that no one will suspect who you really are," he said. "Even so, let me fit ya with this hood."

"I'd recommend you not come near me," she said.

"Is that a threat, now?" said the captain.

"No," she said. "I just strongly recommend you don't take just another step closer to me."

"And what if I did?" He slowly slid his bulk forward as a blur of cerulean came from above and knocked him on his teeth.

Gord and Lew slackened their grip as they turned to see Cross-Time Coordination Agent Lovejoy landing her fists in their faces.

I worked myself free of the cords tying me to the Christmas tree.

"Lovejoy," I said, "It's always a pleasure, but this time even more so."

"Ishmael," she replied, "what the devil are you doing here? You can't be here right now."

"Now you tell me," I said. "I intended to be here three months ago, but taco boy burped and everything went to hell. What are you doing here?"

"Something you can't know about as it would violate the Law of Trans-Temporal Consanguinity, which, for some reason, only applies to you. Needless to say, get yourself to another time point now."

"I'd love to," I said, "but I have a couple of problems with that. One, some usurper asshole has taken control of my little town, and I'd like to see that control go into other hands."

"Mine, perhaps," said Lizzabits.

"Perhaps," I said. "Or anyone from Wal who isn't going to stoop to murder and Christmas Burnings to consolidate their power."

"I'm sorry," said Lovejoy, "but bigger things are afoot. Things that you're really not supposed to be around for."

"I'd love to leave," I said, "but we come to my second big problem with all of this: I have no idea where my method went."

"Your watch?" said Lovejoy.

"It's gone," I said. "I can't explain it."

"Then I'll just have to take you to HQ myself."

Lovejoy is what those in the time travel community call a Natural. Her ability to flash between time points is inborn. And she's had a lot of practice. She's one of the few time travelers I've met who can take a passenger with her.

She put her hand on my shoulder, a move of hers that is hard to resist in both the best and the worst of times. I figured I might as well prepare myself for another creeped out meeting with the Orb at CTCAHQ. The flash began, and the world was filled with a fuzzy kind of purple light. But, somehow, it didn't take.

Instead of a non-stop flight back to the time of chimpanzees, all that happened to us was a moment of temporary paralysis.

That moment was all that was needed for the, now recovering, heavy thugs to grab us and tie us to our trees. It's one of the most difficult, embarrassing, and vulnerable feelings in the world to be lashed to a try while you're physically unable to move. I know worse things have happened to people, and I don't want to make light of any of that. On the other hand, we were in very real danger of being lit on fire. In fact, it was beginning to seem pretty inevitable.

Lovejoy was the first to speak as our faculties came back to us.

"What the devil's going on here?"

"If I didn't know any better," I groaned, "I'd say it was some fiendishly devised trap for time travelers. But who the hell would set it in Wal? I'm the only one who comes to Wal."

"Not so, Ishmael Fugit," said Lizzabits. "There is another. There has always been another. From your family. He just asks us not to tell you about him."

"Gramps?" I said.

"Well," said Lovejoy, "it looks like we may get a chance to see what happens when the Law of Trans-Time Consanguinuity is violated after all."

"Too much talking, my little Christmas tree angels," said the captain of the heavies. "Gord! Lew! Gag these three quiet till it's show time."

Chapter 16
Blood and Feathers

(*Larry*)

So, I crapped my pants, but even I'm not sure if that was literally or figuratively, as I'd been mucking about in a sewer all day, so it was pretty hard to tell where things began or ended. The one thing that was for sure was that there were more damned talking dinosaurs in my life.

We were pretty much surrounded by these demented turkey looking things that, I guess, are what velociraptors *actually* look like. Feathers on them, too. And they were giggling like a chorus of kindergartners juiced up on pixie sticks on Halloween.

In the end, it's the sounds the dinosaurs make that really gets me. And the fact that they talk. And that the big one, way bigger than the velociraptors, but not as big as the allosaur that wasted Agent Hastings back in San Diego. Anyway, this big one was wearing a red and white striped sweater and aviator glasses like he was trying to pull of his best Tom Cruise dressed as Where's Waldo impression. I mean, I might as well be looking at one of those Cthulhus that the weird kid in my high school English class was always talking about. I mean, screw that kid. This right here, a 9 foot utahsaurus in a Hannah Anderson sweater, that is the most unspeakable of unspeakable horrors I could imagine.

Which is why my pants were thoroughly greased inside and out.

Apparently Queequeg owed this dinosaur's boss some money, which was a whole other level of mind-eff for me. Are these, like, mobster dinosaurs or something?

I was out of my depth and pretty sure I was going to die. I mean, I'd seen a lot of crazy stuff since I'd started time traveling with Ishmael. But, I always had Ishmael there to watch my back. Plus, at the beginning, I was pretty wasted and didn't really know what was going on.

But now, at this point, befouled and cowering in the snow with a crotchety old fart who, let's face it, probably could give a shit and a half about my sorry ass, I was pretty sure I was going to be eaten by several dinosaurs.

And then the big one started talking again, in a voice that sounded like some kind of industrial machinery trying to make love to a school bus:

"What makes you think your privileged timeline has any bearing on me whatsoever?" it said.

"Well," said Queequeg. "You're welcome to try your worst. I'm just not very confident it will turn out the way you're planning."

The old mad was bluffing. I'm pretty sure. I have no idea what this 'privileged timeline' b.s. is, but I'm pretty sure it's b.s.

"It doesn't matter," said the dinosaur. "Horkachorge wants you alive. He's just not particular on whether you still have all your limbs attached when I deliver you."

"And what about the kid?" Queequeg asked.

"We could eat him," said the utahsaurus. Then the dinosaur turned his creepy, Tom Cruise aviator shades toward me and asked, "but have you smelled yourself, lately? What you've been marinating in is not very appetizing, to say the least."

"Um, thanks," I said.

The little, creepy velociraptors started laughing again, and a bunch of them pelted me with snowballs. Not only are they creepy as all hell, they're total a-holes.

"So," said Queequeg, "what say you turn the little stinkpot loose, and I'll go with you quietly."

Even I wasn't buying that line. All the dinosaurs started laughing, and I kind of joined them.

Then there was this other noise, kind of like a kid pretending to be a racecar. It's not the kind of noise I should have been able to hear, but it was really loud, like the kid was really, really into pretending to be a racecar. And then I saw what was making it.

It was that Cooper guy, running hell for leather away from the main part of the ruins of the K-Mart the town was built in. He was headed straight for us in this loping, wild man gait that somehow kept him from getting bogged down in the snow. I think we were all kind of like, 'what the eff is this guy doing?'

It was almost like he was running as though he couldn't see us, because, there he was, making his *rrrreeeeeeeoowwwwnnn* racecar noise and making straight for the bulk of the dinosaurs, straight for the big guy. Obviously the guy had no idea what he was looking at. Or maybe he just didn't care.

"What the eff is this guy doing?" I said, because somebody had to.

And what Cooper did was, in three strides, he hopped up, on top of, and over the utahsaurus with the sweater. And then he bolted into the woods behind it.

And that was the moment. The heads of every one of those mother flipping dinosaurs, even the big one, turned to watch him in a kind of stunned surprise.

That's when grampy Queequeg dislocated my shoulder as he dragged me out of the snow. Yeah, it hurt, but I knew it was our only moment and we had only one possible plan: run like hell for Hannie's Hostel.

Running like hell was easier said than done, as we had to aim our feet for the tracks in the snow we'd made earlier. Those were walking strides, not running strides. Now it was like running for your life through one of those stupid obstacle courses with all the tires laid out on the ground. Only the tires are made of ice.

Luckily, the big dinosaur had a worse time of it than we did. His body was even less adapted for a cold weather climate. He stepped gingerly through the snow as every forward movement brought his abdomen right up against the wet, cold, unpleasantness. It explained the sweater, though.

The little velociraptors, on the other hand, were light enough to stay on top of the snow. They skittered across the post-apocalyptic frozen parking lot like turkeys from hell.

I could see Hannie's. We were getting closer, but I was seriously doubting whether I'd be able to get in the door before those laughing little bastards took me down like a diseased caribou.

Then I heard the racecar noise again. And the barking of dogs.

Coming along side us were Cooper and a pack of the rangiest looking mutts I'd ever seen. Not an AKC pedigree worth noting in the bunch. If anything, they looked like light-weight hyenas, but they weren't laughing.

The little velociraptors weren't laughing either.

The dogs started tearing into those creepy effing dinosaurs like I was having a Jack London induced fever dream. The snow was covered in barking, blood, and feathers. My ears were ringing with Cooper's racecar *rrrreeeeeeeeoowwwwwnnn*. And the tide was definitely turning.

The weird thing was I don't think the dogs were even there to help us out. When we got to the door of Hannie's, I turned around to see that Cooper and his pack of wild hounds were heading toward the main building of Wal, leaving the twitching, crumpled bodies of the velociraptors where they'd fallen.

"How the hell did that work out?" I asked.

"Privileged timeline," said Queequeg as he pushed open the door.

"You Fugits and your privileged timeline," said a voice from inside. A familiar voice. A voice that I had only ever heard in a sort of superior and annoyed tone. Pretty much the same tone it had right now. But I was surprised to hear it.

"Hastings," I said. "I thought you were dinosaur chow."

"And I thought you were being babysat by the other Fugit," said Hastings.

"Ishmael? Where is he, anyway?" I said.

"Not in the same room with Queequeg," said Hastings. "In fact, he's not even supposed to be in the same chronopoint. We're looking at a serious paradox potential here."

"Cool your shorts, Hastings," said Queequeg. "I know what I'm doing."

"I don't think you do," said Hastings.

About this point, I noticed there was something else in the room lurking behind Hastings, blending into the shadows. It was person shaped, but smaller, kind of monkey sized. Before I got a really good look, it jumped up into the rafters.

"Okay," I said, "I'll admit there's a lot of shit I don't understand, but what the eff is that thing?"

Everyone turned around and looked, but none of them had an answer. Whatever the little guy was, it seemed to be pointing a ninja sword at me. What a day.

Chapter 17
The Things You Think About
While Tied to a Christmas Tree

(Ishmael)

I am certain that there exist textiles and materials that are more comfortable to the wearer when they are used as a gag. There have to be. There are whole industries built up around that sort of thing. However, none of said comfortable materials existed in Wal.

Whatever it was the heavies had shoved in my mouth, it was largely unidentifiable. Except for the bits with fur. There were definitely bits with fur. Or, maybe lichen. No, lichen wouldn't have seemed as greasy. It had to be fur.

At least trying to decode the mystery of the gag provided distraction from the chafing of the rough cords that bound me to my 'Christmas tree.'

I'd felt a glimmer of hope earlier when Agent Lovejoy had come charging in like the cavalry. But now that hope had been dashed, crushed, and beaten to a pulp by the fact that even her method wasn't working. What good are time travelers who can't time travel?

Now she was tied to her own tree a few paces away. A few paces on the other side of me was Lizzabits. We were all destined to be part of Wal's inaugural tree lighting ceremony, fondly known in other towns as a Christmas Burning.

Now, I don't know what it says about me as a person, but ever since I began the life of a time traveling chronocacher, I'd always come back to Wal. One of my very first jumps into the future was to see the Crash. I was the kind of kid who, growing up, I knew it was coming. Try as I might to hide from the facts I could see that the great bubble that was human civilization, especially the American variety, was due to burst.

Many a night I wished I could have been as oblivious as Larry. I took an honest stab at drinking away the knowledge, but it always came back the next day, like a Quaker with a vengeance.

When great-great gramps handed me the watch, I knew that, as soon as I'd gotten my legs traveling to the known elements of the past, I'd have to pop ahead a bit to see the future. First I'd take a peek at some lotto numbers. Then I'd find the moment when civilization finally loses its gusto and falls in on itself.

It wasn't as soon as I'd feared, but it was there. And it was as awful as you could imagine.

But, for all the horrors I saw, I realized there was hope. The circumstances might have been absolute shit, but people still had the stubborn drive to rise above it.

In a lot of cases it turned out that a strongman bully would consolidate some power for a while, murder and pillage his way to a certain amount of domination over a few square miles, and live like a king till he ran out of ammunition. Then another bully would show up and start a new predictable cycle.

I was glad that the rampaging cannibal horde thing didn't really catch on. There were a couple instances, but they never lasted for long. The people who turn to cannibalism as their first resort tend to have trouble staying organized. Something about trust issues, I suppose.

What I did see was that, with a little preparation, foresight and positioning, things didn't have to be absolutely terrible.

So I took my lotto winnings and invested in a strip mall anchored by a big box retailer. Then I made sure that certain resources, certain knowledge, and certain pieces of advice were available when needed. I was kind of a poor man's Hari Seldon, I suppose. Wal was no

Foundation, but it was an island of relative civility in a post-apocalyptic barbarian world. And the solar panels worked great for the first twenty years.

As I returned time and again to counsel the Storemasters, my biggest, most strenuously worded piece of advice was to not jump on the human sacrifice bandwagon.

Now some usurper bully had come in and found it fitting to light me up on a Christmas tree.

So, I was pretty much stewing, wondering where it had all gone wrong, and trying to figure out how to spit out the furry gym sock that was stuffed in my mouth. The heavies working for the usurper asshole were gone. Probably off to happy hour. Which was why I was left to such horrid rumination and just a touch of self-pity. I really didn't want to be lit on fire, and I really hated being stuck in a situation in which all I could do was contemplate its imminent occurrence.

Of course, as in many such situations where you find yourself tied to a drying conifer, other things were going on outside my immediate sphere of awareness. Behind me something was happening. Someone cut the ropes tying me in place. As soon as my hands were free I tore the gag out of my mouth. I turned and saw Lovejoy stepping away from her own tree, newly freed. She hadn't cut my ropes, but who?

Not Lizzabits. She was still firmly secured and ready for immolation.

It took several attempts at spitting out what was left of the squirrel pelt that had been shoved in my mouth before I could make any words come out.

"Who?" was all I could manage.

"I'm not alone," she said. "This is a big operation."

"Orb?" I asked

"It's pathetic how poorly you handle being gagged," she said, dodging my question. "Let's go before Gord and Lew return."

"Not," I said, taking pause to spit out some more loose fur. "Not without Liz."

"We don't have time."

"No, we're time travelers. The one thing we do have is time. Listen, the people in this town are under my protection. Lizzabits is one of my people and I am not going to let some usurper asshole light her on fire for Christmas. That's not the way we do things in Wal."

"Oh my god," said Lovejoy. "That *must* be it. You've criss-crossed your timeline all through this place. I can see it now. That's why I couldn't flash you out of here. You've knit yourself into the temporal fabric of this town."

"Sounds about right," I said, as I loosened Liz's ropes.

"I know you like to bend the Laws of Time," said Lovejoy, "but when you bend so many at once, some of them are going to snap."

"Lovejoy," I said, "since when has CTCAHQ given half a crap about what happens after the Crash?"

"If you had taken the invitation and become an agent," she said, "you'd know."

I finally got Lizzabits away from her tree and the squirrel gag out of her mouth.

"Thanks for the rescue," she said, "but I'm not going to kiss you."

"Don't flatter yourself, squirrel breath. Any idea how we can get out of here?"

Lovejoy made some hand gestures toward the top of the wall that Cooper had gone over earlier. Some shadowy figures, rather small shadowy figures, flitted about and returned some gestures of their own.

"Well," said Lovejoy, "they won't be much help. They say this fight isn't theirs."

"There's another fight going on?" I said.

"Yes," said Lovejoy. "You didn't honestly think the Agency gave half a crap about the micro-politics of your little toy town, did you?"

"You know, Lovejoy, you're being so less than helpful that not even the jumpsuit's doing it for me right now."

"Right," she said. "I may be back. You're important for some reason."

And with that, Lovejoy flashed out of Wal leaving Lizzabits and me to figure out our own escape.

"Ishmael," said Lizzabits, "I don't like your friend."

"Yeah, well, she's not really a friend. More like somebody that I used to know."

The shadows at the top of the wall scurried and dipped away from view. Were they holding little swords? What was going on? I was so clueless I was starting to feel like Larry on a day ending in 'y.'

"Any ideas?"

"We could always slip out through the piss grate," she said, pointing to a storm drain in the corner of the courtyard.

"Piss," I said. "Great."

In the distance a din was growing. It was the barking of dogs. The barking of dogs, and what sounded like a little kid making racecar noises. I didn't seem like a noise I wanted to be near.

"Okay," I said. "Let's try the piss grate."

Chapter 18

"If You Saw a Monkey Ninja, It's Because the Monkey Ninja Wanted You To"

(*Larry*)

Nobody answered. They were all being jerks like that. Gramps, Hastings, Hannie. It was like none of them had any respect for a guy who'd crawled out of a sewer and narrowly escaped a pack of creepy-ass mini-dinosaurs.

"Seriously," I said, pointing up into the rafters at the tiny, shadowy ninja-thingie. "What the fuck is that?"

"Watch your language," said gramps. And I could really kick that guy, for the amount of love I was not feeling.

Hastings just ignored me and kept talking to gramps about some timeline crap and busting his chops for bending fifty-seven different Laws of Time. I swear the dude looked like he was about to get out his ticket book and write up some citations. That was kind of funny, but it sure as hell wasn't getting my question answered. And, basically, after having run-ins with velociraptors and wild dogs on that very same day, I really wanted to know if the critter that was sharpening its katana in the trusses was a threat to me.

So, I decided to put some swagger into it. I popped my most sewage encrusted arm around Hastings' shoulder, just like the frat boys do.

"Seriously, bro," I said, "are you going to give me the scoop on the ninja monkey, or what?"

Before I knew it, Hastings had me with my arm twisted around my back and screaming 'uncle' on the floor.

"There's nothing there," he said. "Even if you think you see something, you don't. Got it?"

"You don't have to be such a dick about it," I said. "You can just admit that you don't know."

"Relax, Larry," said Grampy Queequeg. "If you saw a monkey ninja, it's because the monkey ninja wanted you to."

"Queequeg," said Hastings, "you have pushed it far beyond any expectation of reasonable tolerance on my part. Do I have to stop my operation here and take you back to HQ?"

"The kid's right," said Queequeg. "You really don't have to be such a dick."

"I'm not bluffing," said Hastings.

"You're bluffing," said Queequeg. "If we've got an Observer in the rafters — by the way, Larry, that little guy's an Observer, but that's all I can tell you about him — like I was saying, if we've got an Observer in the rafters, this scene is too hot for you to leave. So, I'm thinking it might be nice if you toned down the dick attitude and enlightened us a bit about what's going on?"

"Well, Queequeg," said Hastings, "for some reason there is a talking dinosaur crime syndicate setting up shop here in the twilight days of the humanity. It's a serious violation of basic continuity law that needs to be addressed. Talking dinosaurs in 1993 California is one thing, but here? So close to the Great Time Barrier? You wouldn't happen to know anything about that, would you?"

"Actually," said Gramps, "it might have a little bit to do with some bad blood between me and an allosaur named Horkachorge."

"We've met," said Hastings.

"No shit," I said. "That guy tore you up. How did you survive that?"

"Let's just say I wasn't supposed to die yet," said Hastings. "And now I have something specifically horrifying to look forward to when I do."

"I still don't get it," I said, "but, whatever..."

"Waldo will probably be here any minute," said Queequeg.

"Waldo?" said Hastings.

"You'll see," said Queequeg.

It was pretty much about then that the door crashed open and that one dinosaur with the sweater barged himself in.

"That's him," said Queequeg as he flipped a table on it's side and took cover behind it. Lacking any better ideas, I joined him.

"I should have known you'd be on a first name basis with our prime suspect here," said Hastings as he joined us.

Somehow Waldo, the dinosaur, suavely removed his mirrored sunglasses like he actually was Maverick in *Top Gun*. Don't ask me how he managed to pull it off with his little dinosaur arms. He just did. I guess he's super flexible, but he still totally looked like Tom Cruise. And, suddenly, I stopped being so scared of Waldo, and I just started hating him for being a prick. And I'm not sure the red and white stripped sweater was working for him anymore, now that the front part was sagging from his belly and dripping with snow.

"A timecop?" said Waldo. "You involved a timecop? You know, my boss ate a timecop once."

"Only I didn't go down so well," said Hastings. He's sure one cocky mother trucker.

Now, up till this point I hadn't been paying much attention to Hannie, because she was mostly off doing what I assume are parts of her job. She's a business owner in her establishment. She has stuff to take care of. But, now that there was a dinosaur was threatening to bust up her fixtures, she took a more active role in the proceedings.

Basically, she unloaded a shotgun on Waldo, totally shredding his sweater.

"That one was rock salt," she said. "Next one's buckshot. I suggest you leave my establishment before I use it."

"Buckshot," he said. "That's for those soft, furry mammals that slide down the throat without much chewing, isn't it? I think I'll be fine."

Hannie unloaded again, and that sweater was totally history. Waldo, though, was taking it in stride. He made a run for Hannie, but he was on her turf. She ducked into the kitchen and bolted the door behind her. A moment later, her trusty shotgun barrel made an appearance in the pass-through window.

It gave me pause to think that this might actually be a cool restaurant to work at. The adrenaline must have been kicking in again.

Anyway, after that, what went down in Hannie's Hostel kind of came through as a jumble of moments and instances. Pretty much your standard action movie fight scene montage kind of thing, so I'm just going to throw it all out there like that. Feel free to set it to the any butt-rock anthem of your choice.

So, goes without saying that Waldo starts going apeshit, tearing up the joint in pursuit of Grampy Queequeg. It was pretty obvious Queequeg was the primary target. I mean, Waldo pretty much stepped over me like I wasn't there.

Hastings got a couple shots off with a little laser gun thing, but I don't think they more than tickled the big guy.

Hannie kept filling the air with buckshot, which was more than a little nervous-making, because, what with the dinosaur trashing about, everyone was in motion, looking for cover, and jamming out to Europe's "Final Countdown" in our heads.

And then those creepy, disgusting, possessed-kindergarten-giggling-sounding velociraptors showed up. I guess not all of them turned into puppy chow when that pack of wild dogs tore through earlier. So, seriously, we're in a confined space, scrambling to get away from all kinds of dinosaurs when this happens:

A bunch of the shadowy things drop out of the ceiling. And, no shit, they are ninja monkeys. They have swords. They have ninja suits. And they had one more thing.

I was close enough to hear as one said, in what was a pretty legit robot voice, "engaging threat-level anachronistic bipeds."

Robot. Monkey. Ninjas.

It was on. These guys were all over the velociraptors. Wings and drumsticks were flying everywhere as they put their little katanas to work. They seemed to totally ignore Waldo, though, besides gingerly ninja flipping out of his way as he crashed after Queequeg. But this totally didn't make sense, because those creepy little turkeys are stupid. Waldo had the brawn and the brains, so it would make sense to go after him. But, obviously, nothing was making sense.

Which is when there was a flash of blue and, suddenly, Agent Lovejoy was next to me. Which is cool because, a) she's hot, and b) she kicks some serious ass.

"And I thought things were bad with Ishmael," she says. Then she pulls out this ridiculously huge gun and joins the dance.

Speaking of dance partners, that's when three more of these Waldo-sized utahsauruses came in. I don't know where these guys got their fashions sense, but these guys were decked out something weird. One had a bomber jacket, another a trench coat, and the third was wearing one of those Lycra bicycling get ups like he'd just been training for the Tour de France. Let me tell you, it was quite the tableau.

At this point, these guys were just going for anything. Tour de France was this close to taking a bite out of my head when a robot voice said "preserve Larry."

All of the sudden, half a dozen of the ninja monkeys had formed a pyramid between me and the utahsaur. Katanas were flying and it was the absolute perfect time for me to make for the exit.

Out in the snow again, I find Queequeg had slipped out of the fray as well. He was standing there messing with his watch. I figure he'd decided it was time to bug out, but he bothered to depart a little bit out wisdom before his exit.

"Here's the deal with me and the dinosaurs," he said. "In case nobody manages to figure it out. Horkachorge, the boss, is pissed at me for chronocaching his brother's carcass in a silty lake bottom. I made a killing off those fossils on the gem show circuit, and Horkachorge has been bitter ever since. A little bit because he was upset about his brother, who died of *natural* causes, but mostly because I didn't cut him in. But he's a dinosaur, and money doesn't travel backwards. Besides, I spent it all."

All this while, Hannie's Hostel was crumbling from the rumble inside. It was starting to look even more structurally unsound by the minute. Also, a weird blue glow was starting to creep out of every crack and fissure.

"Well," said Queequeg, "it looks like CTCAHQ and their monkey friends have this in hand. I'm going to go run a few errands."

He hit the button on his watch and, instead of me seeing him flash out of existence before my eyes, I saw everything flash out of existence. Great, I thought, now I'm stuck traveling with gramps.

Only, when the world came back, gramps wasn't there. But Ishmael was, and this chick, who, I got the feeling would clean up really nice. But who was I to judge? I was more painfully aware than ever that I hadn't had a minute to change clothes since traipsing through sewage all day.

And there we were, in the middle of some junked up courtyard with three of the saddest looking Christmas trees I'd ever seen.

It was then that I noticed there was something in my hand.

"Dude," I said, "why do I have your watch?"

Chapter 19
Whether I'm What?

(*Larry*)

Honestly, sometimes I don't know if I am right now, or if I'm five years ago or if I'm already somewhere I'm planning to go later this afternoon. These are just moments. Just brief spots of looking up and realizing I have no idea how long I've been on the Interstate and maybe, just maybe, I was supposed to take Exit 57 and I don't know if I'm on the bit where the exits count up or count down, but, look out, here comes Exit 59.

I suppose it could be easy to explain it away as a side effect of time travel. Or too many nickel pitcher nights at the Salty Dawg. But, truthfully, I think I was always like this. I just space out.

So it wasn't too hard to just roll with it when, all of the sudden, I was absolutely somewhere I'd never been before looking at a someone I did know and someone else that I didn't know. It was the someone I didn't know that was making me lose my equilibrium a bit.

"How the hell did you get my watch?" said Ishmael. He's the guy I did know.

"No clue, bro," I said. "One second Grampy Queequeg was telling me he was about to bail, and the next second, well, the next second is this second... or a couple seconds ago. Is there a real quantifiable difference between the immediate past and the absolute present, anyway?"

"Stop trying to sound smart," said Ishmael. "It just makes you look stupid."

He grabbed the watch out of my hand, which, for some reason reminded me of how long it had been since I'd had anything to eat. Or shower. Which was suddenly kind of important because the person I didn't know was an absolutely gorgeous punk rock goddess of a girl within an appropriate approximate age range of myself. I mean, you had to account for some cultural drift, because, they probably didn't know what punk rock was out there in the future, so the look was probably totally coincidental. But coincidences can be amazing, man. Oh, they can be the best. And here I was, trying to be cool, trying not to stare, trying not to be a total ass, because you really only have one opportunity to make a first impression, right? Of course, first impressions carrying the kind of weight they do, the only real shot I had at this point was to try and talk a good game. Because, literally, I smelled like shit.

"Dude," I said, "do you have any idea what kind of crap I've had to crawl through to try and rescue you today?"

"Probably similar to the kind of crap we're going to crawl through once we pry that piss grate open," he said, pointing to a rusted storm drain cover in the floor of the courtyard.

"Hold on," I said. "Are we still in Wal? Because if we're still in Wal, you do not want to go into those sewers."

"Why not?" said the girl (Lizzabits, let's not pretend I'm not telling this from a later time, future me knows she's Lizzabits, Ishmael know's she's Lizzabits, you know she's Lizzabits, unless you're worse at keeping track of this story than I am. In which case, surprise! It's Lizzabits, the old Storemaster's daughter. And she's definitely cuter than Ishmael probably let on). "You're already dressed for it."

"I don't suppose you've smelled yourself, lately," I said, because there was really no graceful way to come back to someone telling you that you literally look like shit. This first impression thing was already going horribly wrong. The only thing to do was fall back on whatever it is I am and hope it all works out. But man, I would have killed not to be dressed like a sewer urchin right then.

"Shitten clothes aside," said Ishmael. "What's wrong with the piss grate option?"

"The sewers are filled with some creepy fucking little dinosaurs," I said.

"I thought you were watching your language."

"Seriously, Ish, these are some creepy little fuckers."

"We have to do something," said Lizzabits. "The next people through that door are set upon lighting us on fire."

At that point it was already too late to start doing anything. Some big, fat, Conan the Barbarian villain wannabes came through the door. We wouldn't have had time to scoot down the storm drain, anyway.

"Stokes," said Liz, with this kind of pissed off venom to her voice that let everybody know she really wanted this dude dead in a severely immediate way.

"You've come loose from your tree," said the leader of these guys. I'm guessing he was Stokes. "How can we celebrate the season if our tree's not properly trimmed before we light it?"

"I've got a better idea of what you can do with your tree," said Ishmael.

Stokes laughed. It was that hearty, full of himself, conceited, I'm going to enjoy watching you die laugh that the villain always does in the movies. I was getting tired of being laughed at by smug villain types. First the dinosaurs, now this asshole.

"Bro," I said, "I have no idea who you are, but I've had an unbelievably shitty day, and I'd like to just collect my friends and go. You don't happen to have any tacos, do you?"

"Gord, Lew" said Stokes, "taco this kid when you tie him to his tree." Apparently taco means something different in the future.

Those big guys started making their way toward us, in that slow, menacing, deliberate way that your stereotypical murderous mountain men move. Or maybe they were moving slowly because I smelled so bad. I wouldn't fault them on that. But, I'm also not sure they smelled much better.

"Get the girl first," said Stokes. He was the alpha asshole. Having just stepped in, I had no idea what the micro-politics of the situation were, I just always tend to know who the biggest asshole in the room is.

Speaking of assholes, I wasn't too aware of what Ishmael was doing at that point. Playing with his watch, or something. He was probably fixing to jet just like his grandpa.

I thought, screw him, and planted myself between the man-mountain mountain men and Lizzabits. If it was a foregone conclusion that I was going to get my ass kicked. One way or another, a beat down was coming my way and I saw it. However, if I was going to have to have my ass kicked, I was going to do it in a way that had the highest chance of me impressing a girl.

So there I was, trying to stand like a tough guy as these dudes who outweighed me by at least 300 pounds approached. And now they were giggling. So I started giggling back, because, seriously, every asshole in history was laughing at me today. There was nothing to do to deflect it but join in it.

"It really is pretty funny," I said. "Because god knows who's going to lose a nut between the time you've started with me and the time you've moved on to her. Because, mark my words, someone's losing a nut. Maybe two." And I just started laughing like the craziest asshole I could imagine, which is my roommate Steve. Steve's one of those guys who turns old furniture legs into knives and talks about how he used to hunt feral cats in high school. He's pretty full of shit, but no one messes with him. "And by nut, I do mean gonad."

These guys weren't so impressed. In fact, they both pulled out these crazy looking knives that looked like they'd been made out of dismantled folding chairs by deranged Trekkies. It occurred to me that them and Steve would probably get along.

"How many nuts *you* got?" said one of the guys. "It's time to ante up."

And more of the laughing. It was pretty obvious that whatever was about to go down between me and these guys was going to hurt. Or it would have if what happened next hadn't happened.

Let me back up a little bit, first. All that while, as I was talking tough and wondering what the eff Ishmael was doing just playing with his watch, I saw these little shadowy figures skittering around the top of the wall. They looked a lot like the robot monkey ninjas from Hannie's, but I didn't want to make any assumptions. Especially, since my older brother drilled that old saying into me at an early age, *when I assume, I make you think I'm an ass.*

So, I was really half-posturing, half-wondering if these guys were the cavalry, as I was talking my big talk. But, mostly, I had it figured I had nothing left to lose. And if these big guys were really going to take me down, I was going to take some testicles with me. As gross as it seemed, it was really the least I could do.

And then the wicked folding chair knives came out. And I noticed something different going on with the shadows. They suddenly all had glowing green eyes. That's when I was pretty sure the monkey ninjas were at least partly robot.

"All right, bubs," I said, "bring it on. But you gotta get through me before you get to... uh, what's your name?"

That's when I got hit with the blunt end of one of the folding chair/knife/*bat'leth* things the mountain man guys were wielding. It caught me in the side and, I'm not going to lie, it put me in the dirt right away. It was part of my plan to be on the ground. My plan mainly being: roll with the first punch, then honey badger for the nads.

However, I never even had a chance to put the second part of my plan in action.

A storm of robot monkey ninjas came raining from the courtyard walls. They were all over the mountain man thug guys and that guy

Stokes. Just beating on them with this lighting fast monkey punches and monkey kicks. If George Lucas was there, he could probably base a whole new *Star Wars* trilogy on that epic monkey ninja fight. These guys were badder than the baddest-ass Ewoks in *Jedi*.

I wish I could have seen more of the action, but, instead I was busy checking in on Lizzabits. A lesser guy might have used the atmosphere of danger as an excuse get close enough for one of those Han and Leia moments from *Empire* where, oops, we accidentally fall into each other and maybe accidentally kiss. But, by this time she already had one of those folding chair knives in her hands and she was taking a defensive position over me as I was trying to make my diaphragm remember how to make those breathing movements.

I really hadn't rolled with the mountain man's punch as well as my original plan required. New plan: gasp for air and hope to survive.

Lying on the ground, looking up at her with that tender regard a combination of high adrenaline and low oxygen levels in the blood can inspire in a person, I was ready to propose marriage. She was gorgeous in spite of the sweat and filth of a post-apocalyptic life devoid of shampoo and indoor plumbing, maybe even because of it. She was also becoming surrounded by a dome built entirely of robot monkey ninja acrobats. If that one French-Canadian 'circus' didn't have a thing against performing animals, they would have totally hired these guys. Pure professionalism and grace.

As the monkeys completed their dome formation over me and Lizzabits, they started glowing. First it was in the eyes. Then the glow went from green to blue. Kind of almost that blue of those top shelf gins some dudes put in spray bottles so they can look like they're drinking Windex while they're cruising around town. Then that blue glow spread to other parts, their hands, the joints of their arms and legs, everything in between, until everything was glowing blue.

I closed my eyes against the brightness, and the blue was still the only thing I saw.

Then, as the blue built until an intensity I was sure would make my head explode, I felt that familiar slightly drunk feeling that comes with time travel. We'd flashed somewhere. Somewhere warmer. Somewhere that didn't stink. Even I didn't stink anymore, which was weird, because, as has been documented, I'd bathed in sewage that day.

When I opened my eyes to check out the surroundings, I had to close them again right away. Because, first, the entire surroundings were that same featureless blue color. Even though I was lying on something, the ground was exactly the same color as the sky, which was exactly the same color as the everything else. All I could see was blue. It felt like every single thing was the sky and that, no matter how I twisted or turned, I was falling into it.

Actually, there was one thing else I could see distinct from the blue. Actually, not a thing, but a person. Actually, Lizzabits. And seeing her helped explain why nothing stank anymore and why I was feeling a slight breeze in my scrotal area.

She was naked. I was naked. We both were naked. It wasn't exactly the entire scenario I was hoping for this event to occur in. Life was definitely giving me some weird lemonade.

"Usually," I said, "usually, when I time travel, the clothes come with."

I brought myself into a crotch obscuring crouch and looked off into the distance.

Lizzabets giggled. I don't think she was looking off into the distance.

"It's good to know you're not a wether," she said.

"Whether I'm what?" I asked.

"A wether," she giggled, "a castrated he-goat. It's good to know you're not one."

"I..." I was at a loss. "I was hoping to buy you a drink or two before we got to this whole naked together part."

"Don't flatter yourself," she said. "I'm not so easily swept off to the hayricks. It would take more than a *couple* drinks."

"While you're pouring 'em," interjected an older, more bitter voice, "I could use more than a couple drinks, myself."

I turned, and, yep, it was Ishmael, naked as the rest of us. And that's when I really had to close my eyes again.

Chapter 20
Paradise Lost and Found

SOMEWHEN IN THE MID 1980s of a mid-size city that was situated somewhere in, roughly, the western third of the continental United States was a rundown residential hotel known as the Paradise Arms. The Paradise Arms was, curiously, a wooden building, and after some eighty years of operation, had some curious issues with the foundation, the plumbing, the wiring, the carpet, and just about everything else. There was not a level surface to be found within the building and, seen from the outside, it looked as though the architectural plans had been drawn up by a lonely third grader who didn't have a ruler. Or Edward Hopper with astigmatism. Take your pick.

It was a bit of a miracle that the building hadn't caught fire yet. No one was more surprised at this fact than the residents of the Paradise Arms.

Correction, one person was more surprised than the residents. It was Floyd Earnshaw, the new building manager.

It was a new job for Floyd. He'd been attracted to the old building at first because, being named Floyd, he often felt like he was a man living in the wrong time. He was too young to have been named after Pink Floyd and old enough to sincerely hope he hadn't been named after Floyd the barber from the Andy Griffith Show.

Floyd had been hired on after the old building manager had suddenly vacated the position after an attempted murder on the premises. He'd not only vacated the position, but also the city, and the contents of the cash box in which a significant portion of that month's rent had been collected.

Some people know when to cut and run, thought Floyd.

After accepting the job, Floyd met a few of the residents, and immediately took to wondering if he might not have made a huge mistake. It became obvious that the second floor's studio apartments, with the communal bathrooms down the hall, were the sorts of places intravenous drug users liked to spend their final days.

The apartments on the first floor were no picnic, either. Floyd had the distinct impression that the income of at least one of the first floor residents was largely made up of the proceeds from selling drugs to the people upstairs.

And then there were the dedicated drunks. At least you always knew where they stood. Or leaned. Or vomited. Because they were usually quite loud about it.

The more Floyd thought about his new work environment, the more he thought he could go for a drink himself. It was half past two. So far that day, he'd unstopped two toilets and, temporarily, solved the riddle of one leaky gas stove. There was a bar nearby, and he could surely sneak away for a half hour, but what he'd really like to do is sneak off to a bar quite far away. For that, he'd have to wait another two and a half hours and hope against hope that he wouldn't have to call for emergency services to collect yet another junky nodded out in the upstairs hallway.

Floyd was absolutely surprised that his predecessor hadn't just finished the job and torched the place when he left town with the cash. If that man had any sense of dignity, the building would be a pile of ash and charred timbers and, therefore, not a place in which Floyd could take a job and watch as his will to live left his body breath by breath, drop by beaded drop of sweat.

It was 2:35 and Floyd was debating tracking down the source of a periodic and troubling smell that had been haunting the office. Or he could work on sorting and filing the pile of rental agreements that had been haphazardly strewn about the desk by his predecessor. But that seemed too much like actual work for the last third of the day. Plus, if he took to sorting the paperwork, he might accidentally uncover the source of the smell. If he was going to tackle the smell, he was going to do it intentionally, and with the proper protective equipment, and he really wasn't in the mood to suit up.

So Floyd waited for the phone to ring. It wouldn't. Service had been disconnected as the old building manager hadn't paid the phone bill in four months. But Floyd didn't know that. He hadn't even bothered to check for a dial tone because the receiver appeared to be coated in grease of some sort.

Maybe the phone wouldn't ring.

At 2:37, Floyd no longer had to wonder what he'd do if the phone actually rang, as that is when Queequeg Fugit shoved open the door and stepped into the office.

"Welcome to the Paradise Arms," said Floyd. "Affordable urban living at an affordable price."

"Can it," said Queequeg. "I live here."

"Oh, right," said Floyd. "You'll have to excuse me. I'm new."

"No kidding," said Queequeg. "I need you to check the lost and found for something."

"The lost and found?" Floyd didn't know anything about the Paradise Arms' place for lost and found items. It hadn't been shown to him on his 20 minute orientation. And, honestly, with all the abandoned items of clothing and household goods in the hallway, on the steps, and in the laundry room, it was hard to imagine there was any point in gathering them up to deposit in any location other than the dumpster. "I don't know where that is."

"Figures," said Queequeg. "Bottom drawer of the left-hand filing cabinet."

Floyd turned to check the drawer and stopped short. It was definitely where the smell was coming from. He was sure of it.

"Come on," said Queequeg. "I'm in a hurry."

Floyd came up with a perfectly procedural reason to stall.

"Can you describe the item you are looking for?"

"It's a key," said Queequeg. "A big old skeleton key with a butterfly motif on the handle end."

"Ah," said Floyd. "That's a specific description."

"So hurry up with the checking, please. I've got a pressing engagement."

That was about as much stalling as Floyd felt he could reasonably get away with. He made a second, official approach for the lost and found drawer. The smell was definitely coming from it. It was a smell somewhat reminiscent of the untended grease trap from a restaurant where he once worked as a busboy.

He opened the drawer.

The smell was definitely coming from within.

Floyd gingerly probed contents of the drawer, a heap of sunglasses, wallets, handkerchiefs and socks. Socks? Really?

"I'm afraid I don't see any keys," said Floyd.

"You're not even looking," said Queequeg. "Stir it up a bit."

Floyd thought about stirring through the lost and found drawer and wondered if they made rubber gloves of the sort that were long enough that they'd cover his entire body. It wasn't just the smell anymore. It was the look of some of those socks that was really putting him off.

"Um," said Floyd, "I don't suppose you'd like to take a look for yourself."

"Step aside."

Queequeg approached the drawer, looked at the density of items that had been packed in over some unquantifiable period of time. It appeared as though the lost and found had never been purged on any sort of regular basis, if at all. Queequeg tested the contents and discovered that, below the topmost layer, geological forces were already in the process of fusing the assorted plush animals, hearing aids, and toenail clippers into some obscene new form of igneous rock as the very lower levels of the drawer slowly found themselves becoming something resembling some distant generation's fossil fuel source.

"I wouldn't be surprised if there's a rotten sandwich in there," said Floyd.

"That ain't the half of it."

"Queequeg considered the drawer for a moment. Then he pulled it open as far as it would go before the catch held it in place. He stood up and positioned himself to one side of the drawer, swung his body side to side as a bull readying to charge, then delivered a swift kick.

The drawer pulled loose from the cabinet and scattered its contents across the office floor.

"Hey, now," Floyd protested.

He would have protested more, but what he saw among the flotsam and jetsam of the lost and found drawer gave him pause. More accurately, it gave him full stop with a side of vertigo.

The old man's key was there, for certain. There was no mistaking the old fashioned skeleton key with the stylized butterfly handle. There was also no mistaking that it was still firmly clenched within a maggot eaten fist and an accompanying bit of forearm. The maggots, it seemed, were still having quite a go of it, which means the hand couldn't have been in the drawer for much longer than Floyd's short tenure at the Paradise Arms.

Queequeg set his booted foot down on the wrist and extracted the key from the cold, dead grip that held it. He offered a mumbled word of thanks as he took the key and left.

Floyd needed to take several more moments.

A hand.

A stinking severed hand.

In the lost and found drawer.

Soon he'd be able to actually form a complete sentence. And then he'd have a decent chance at making a proper call to the police. But for the time being all he could handle was stunned stares and sentence fragments.

A certain indistinctly unmeasurable amount of time passed before a voice intruded into Floyd's semi-catatonia.

"Excuse me."

Floyd looked up to see a head at the door. The head was attached to the rest of a man, but it was hard to think of the entire assemblage as a whole. The head was so large that the body seemed to be more of an accessory, rather than an integral part of the outfit. Also, there was a distinct bluish glow coming from the head's delineating features, the eyebrows, the ears, the bridge of the nose, the goatee that really didn't seem to belong on a beach ball like that.

"Are you the building, manager?"

Words were coming back to Floyd. He felt a bit of an endorphin rush as he felt the exact right words fall out of his mouth.

"No, actually," he said. "I was looking for him myself."

Floyd sidled around the giant blue head and out the door. And so Floyd Earnshaw ejected himself from Paradise.

Chapter 21
Naked and Afraid

(*Ishmael*)

This wasn't the first time I'd flashed between time points in the nude. It happens to the best of us. Back when I was a bit more of a socially outgoing member of the time traveling community it was a popular happy hour activity to trade stories of the most embarrassing place you've ended up *au naturel*. They call it pulling a Kyle Reese, or going the full Niffeneggar, or playing the not-so-invisible man.

It tends to happen more often to those who are new to the time traveling game. And more often to those whose method of time travel is inborn rather than tied to a device like a modified Delorean or a 19th century pocket watch. For the inborn, natural time traveler, it can take a while for the *aura effect* to set in to the extent that their clothing joins them on every jaunt. It can be hit and miss and the stories they tell are often hilarious.

My method is the watch. It's a very powerful watch. Gramps had it fully loaded, fully charged, and thoroughly broken in by the time he passed it on to me. Usually, more than usually, pretty much every damn time, my clothes, come with. That is if I'm wearing any when I initiate the time jump. There have been a few moments when one thing led to another and I had to skidoo before I could make myself decent. It happens.

But this time? I don't know how or why this happened.

Lizzabets and I were in Wal trying to figure out the quickest way out of Wal. Then Larry showed up with my watch, apparently as surprised as anyone that he had it. The kid wasn't swift enough to have palmed it on purpose, and, like I've said before, the watch has its way of making sure it stays with me.

So, then, I had the watch in hand, and was trying to figure out just what the hell has gone on with its settings while it's been away, when the local thugs gallery reappeared. I really didn't want to be tied up to ritual human sacrifice Christmas tree for a third time, but I also didn't want to abandon Lizzabits to the thugs. I was trying to see if there might be a way to widen the watch's field enough for three people, when the shadowy figures from the ramparts decided it was time to be active participants.

I really hate to overuse the phrase robot monkey ninjas, but that's really the best descriptor. They were at least partly robot, and monkey sized, and they definitely had the ninja skills. Gord, Lew and whatever other monosyllables the rest of Stokes' crew hailed by were no match for these guys.

The weird part of it all, though, was that the monkeys were clearly protecting Larry. Like he was important or something.

It suddenly occurred to me in a way I had been consciously avoiding, that Larry must have some kind of destiny, some sort of principal role in the tangled unfolding of whatever this chain of events was that involved time cops, talking dinosaurs, robot monkey ninjas, and post-apocalyptic barbarian thugs. I admit that I was more than a bit jealous to realize that Larry just might actually be the hero of this story. Or, perhaps he was the damsel in distress.

In either case, the monkeys were going to bat for him. They formed a perimeter around Larry and Lizzabits, and then did the sort of acrobatic maneuver of the sort you'd expect to see in a cheerleading competition movie. They assembled themselves into a dome four monkeys high. And then the method kicked in. The monkeys were generating a time travel field within the dome.

Larry and Lizzabits were being escorted somewhen. And of course, because my method and Larry's had been so annoyingly linked by the Orb some fifteen chapters back, I had no choice but to follow.

So there we were, full Niffeneggar in the middle of what they call the Great Time Barrier, a time point I had only ever heard about and never travelled to because, honestly, what's the point? You can't move forward, there's nothing to bring back, and everything looks like a migraine.

The totality of the Time Barrier glowed that damned cerulean blue the CTCAHQ boys and girls love so much, a blue that shines with the seething intensity of a time jump that never quite ends. There was nothing really to see except the maddening, unending blue, and the tracers of white blood cells across our retinas. The only distinguishing features were the monkeys that periodically faded into and out of the background.

"Ishmael?" said Larry. "What happened to our clothes? Was it... was it the Greys? Are we on a UFO? Have I been anally probed?"

"If you have," I said, "I had nothing to do with it."

"At least it's warm here," said Lizzabits. "And I'll thank the two of you to keep your eyes askance."

"And I'd just like to apologize ahead of time," said Larry. "There's a bit of a breeze catching at a certain spot so, if I might appear to be at half-mast, it's nothing personal. No offense."

"None taken," I said.

"I wasn't talking to you," said Larry.

"Ah," said Lizzabits. "Maybe I should be taking offense, then, if that's not personal."

"Hey, babe," said Larry, "this 'eyes askance' deal goes both ways so, dammit, don't look. Unless, of course, you want to amend the deal."

"Just what sort of deal do you propose?"

If I'd had a hose, I'd turn it on the two of them. As I was listening to their nonsense, a shape began to resolve itself in the impossible to judge distance. Something was moving in the blue. Something that was picking up speed.

"Holy shit," said Larry. "Another dinosaur. Look at the size of it..."

I was trying to gauge the size of it for myself. It didn't seem that big but, not having any reference points to compare it to, I decided to err on the side of caution.

"We'd better run for it," I said.

Larry and Lizzabits got right on board with that plan, but not without some unnecessary whinging from Larry.

"Running's only making my half-mast situation worse!"

"I swear to god, Larry, I do not need to hear about your 'half-mast situation.'"

It turned out that running didn't matter much. Our pursuer was much closer, and much smaller than I had imagined.

"Crap," said Larry. "Another velociraptor."

"You sure?" I asked, as the bipedal scavenger gained on us.

"Dead sure," said Larry. "I've been running from these guys all day."

I desperately scanned out surroundings for some kind of object I could use as a shield or weapon. There was nothing. In every direction, up, down, side to side, nothing distinguished itself from the solid sky blue background. Even the ground was blue. Although ground didn't seem like the right word. Floor doesn't do it justice, either. It was a surface, and we could run across it. Other than that, there weren't any good descriptors for it other than 'blue'. The place was like a low budget existential nightmare. The only things we knew we had for sure wer our own bodies and the prehistoric reptilian terror machine closing in on our asses.

Literally.

I, being older and not so much a runner as I am a plotter, schemer, and hider, couldn't keep up with the pack in our impromptu foot race from the velociraptor. So, I was bringing up the rear, by virtue of shear inability to keep pace with the other two. And it wasn't long before I felt something at my rear. The damned feathered dino was snapping at my buttocks.

That was enough. I stopped dead in my tracks. It wasn't the most graceful of stops. In fact, to the outside observer, it may have looked like I'd involuntarily fallen. Even so, it was a finely calculated fall from which I rolled into a savage crouch on the strange blue not-floor of whenever the hell the Great Time Barrier was.

The velociraptor, with its finely honed lizard-bird reflexes, leaped into the air as to avoid collision.

That's when I had the surprising fortune and good timing to make one of the most dubious decisions of my storied career. As the velociraptor's feathered tail swept over me, I reached up and grabbed it.

Here's a fun fact. Small scavenging dinosaurs apparently were not evolutionarily adapted to protect their tails from being grasped by opposable thumbed primates. Either that or this was the world's dumbest velociraptor.

That I had been able to grab the dinosaur's tail was surprising enough. That it was so easy maintain my grip once I had it blew my mind.

The velociraptor couldn't believe it either. It flailed its legs and creepy, out-sized, terror claws against the not-floor trying to get purchase, trying to return to the chase of its primary target which, evidently, was not me. It took the velociraptor a moment to realize that now was the time for things to turn ugly.

Here's a word of advice, to go with the earlier fun fact. If you ever find yourself in a situation where you're considering engaging in unarmed combat with a dinosaur, don't. Not even the small ones.

I sensed the change in the velociraptor's attention as it ceased to pedal its legs. A distinct differentiation in intent was telegraphed by the change in tension in the muscles of the velociraptor's tail. Things were about to get extra dangerous, and all I had to work with was my bare hands.

I pulled up from my crouch and yanked hard on the beast's tail. Now, I've said before that this was a small dinosaur. In actuality, it was much smaller than the velociraptors Mr. Spielberg depicted in his loud and cinematically curious film. Your actual, real life velociraptor is about the same size as a goose. Having said that, you know how mean geese are? Now imagine an angry goose with teeth and crazy, bowel-shredding talons on their feet and you'll have a good idea of how terrifying it is to have one of these guys by the tail.

I spun the dinosaur like I was an Olympic hammer thrower. Three times around, hoping the centrifugal force and the length of the critter's tail would keep those thrashing talons far enough away from my soft tissues. It worked, at least for the short term. And if I could have kept spinning like that forever I would still be there, but on the fourth turn around my grip gave loose.

The writhing, butterball-sized mass of feathers, teeth, and talons flew a good twelve feet. Decent, but not far enough. I just hoped the little bugger was dizzier than I was.

I made it a few strides before my legs gave way. I felt for the watch. It was still with me, somehow, even though I didn't have a pocket to put it in. I contemplated hitting the emergency default, which would get me and Larry out of danger. But would it take Lizzabits too? And did I really want to show up at CTCAHQ going the full Niffeneggar?

Not really. The Orb was near the top of the short list of people I absolutely never wanted seeing me naked.

But none of that whole chain of decision making process mattered. Before I knew it, Larry was taking a stand right between me and the velociraptor. Have I mentioned that Larry was starting to grow on me? Adrenaline does strange things to your mind, but I almost could have kissed the guy right then.

I pulled myself to my feet. There was no way you could count this as a fair fight. Let's face it, naked humans are pretty pathetic. Our soft and squishy bits would be no match for the raptor's sharp and stabby bits. But maybe it would think twice seeing that we outweighed and outnumbered it.

Apparently it didn't think twice. As soon as the demon turkey recovered from its tumble, it turned toward us, flexing its terrible talons, emitting a soft, deranged kindergartner giggle.

Chapter 22

What to Believe When Everything You've Believed in is Gone

(*Larry*)

People have accused me of not really standing for much in my lifetime, and, to be fair, for the most part that's true. When I was a kid, I was into the usual stuff with the clear cut good guys versus bad guys thing. You know, GI Joe and Cobra, Autobots and Decepticons, Smurfs and Gargamel. It was always comforting and easy to know that you could define yourself as being against something that was clearly mean, bad, and unable to hit the broadside of a barn with an AK-47. Seriously, as often as the Joe team encountered Cobra in close quarters, nobody ever took a bullet.

And suddenly, when I was in high school and starting to realize that, if they reinstated the draft, I was almost old enough for it, the great force opposing the freedom and democracy of the First World, the Soviet Union, evaporated.

All my kid life I was taught that, on the other side of the ocean, there was this evil empire. One day there would be an inevitable confrontation between us and them and I might have to go all *Red Dawn*, or if I was lucky and skilled enough, I could go all *Top Gun*, but either way there would definitely come a time when I'd have to kill the bad guys. Because that's the way America did it, and I was an American and the Russians, with their godless communism and really long lines for bread, or whatever, were our natural enemy.

And then one day it was, like, all the Russian people called bullshit on that, because they were tired of being the bad guys and having to listen to all their Van Halen on crappy bootleg cassettes or something. They wanted to be able to buy the nice stuff, or even just the pretty okay K-mart stuff and they just said screw it, enough of this communism shit.

And with that I was living in a world without good guys and bad guys. And we were all like, what the hell do we do now? What do we stand for? Did we ever really stand for anything other than the right to buy stuff? Because that's what the capitalist thing is all about, on the consumer level, right? We have the freedom to buy whatever we can afford, and whatever we can't afford, we can get on credit. But the hell does that even mean if I can't get a job at the missile plant because there are no more bad guys to shoot missiles at?

And I think that it was in the midst of this general kind of feeling of aimlessness and lack of purpose that Nirvana came in and said "you are absolutely right in thinking all this is pointless."

So, bearing that in mind, I've spent my first few years of adulthood adrift and without any overall sense of purpose. Also, I learned how to drink cheap beer quickly and in mass quantities. As a result, it may seem like I'm an apathetic slacker with no values. But that's not true.

I have at least one core value.

Basically, when shit gets real, you get your friends' backs. That's a value no one can deny. Now, while the nature of our mentor-mentee relationship might strain the traditional boundaries of friendship, Ishmael *was* the best friend I had at the moment. And he was naked and fighting a muther-effing dinosaur.

I had no choice but to help him fight that muther-effing dinosaur.

Plus, there was a girl involved. A girl in my age range who, even though we'd barely just met, had a pretty interesting style about her, considering her whole growing up after the end of civilization thing.

What I'm saying is it wouldn't do me any good to look bad, so I stepped up.

The creepy effing velociraptor had just regained its feet in that strange blue wherever we were. It was like a photo lab processing error. The sky, the ground, anything else that might happen to be there, but you couldn't tell because everything was all exactly the same color. And, to make it all a little extra stupid, there was a blue mist that... forget it. The point is that the only thing I could see was us and this dinosaur as though we were floating in some indistinct sky waiting for the graphics department of some sci-fi pulp publishing house to put us on the cover of one of those paperbacks with the yellow spines. You know what I'm talking about, right? The sword and spaceship fantasy novels from the 70s with the yellow spines and a cover painting of a dude fighting a monster in a vague environment while a mostly naked chick looks mostly helpless. Only Lizzabits was looking like she was down to fight. Otherwise, it was pretty much like that.

So the velociraptor was coming at me and I had no idea what I was going to do. The thing was all claws and feathers and demented giggling. And it was picking up speed.

I dropped into a Wolverine style crouch and was thinking 'SNIKT' while I knew I was on the short end of that stick. My adamantium claws were merely imaginary.

I braced for impact as the mini-monster charged. I thought for half a second about where the best place to put my hands would be. All I came up with were several possibilities for the worst place. It became clear that bracing was probably one of the least useful things I could do and, rather than wait, I went on the offensive.

I started running at the monster and screaming holy hell. My hands were flying in the air like I was some kind of demented Dracula.

As I ran up to meet it, the velociraptor started to backpedal a bit. Just a little bit. And I screamed louder and prepared to jump. This was it. The velociraptor, backpedalling or no, was going to call my bluff and tear my soft fleshy bits into machaca. I was resigned to that fact and, in a way, realizing that I was about to resemble one of my favorite taco fillings was a little comforting.

In the middle of that peaceful fit of acceptance and screaming, the miracle occurred.

Just as the dinosaur and me were about to make contact, a posse of those robot ninja monkeys showed up out of the blue. Literally. They just popped out of the blue fog and turned on the T-U-R-T-L-E power.

There were feathers, a dinosaur scream, and surprisingly little blood. The velociraptor seemed to dissolve like a fallen Jedi. Or maybe he just popped back to the Late Whateverous Period that he came from to escape the fate of an unavoidable ninja death.

Either way, my ass was saved in such a way that I actually did not look like a total chickenshit while doing it.

One of the robot monkeys turned and looked me over. Or looked me through. It was like he was checking every single vital sign with some futuristic tri-corder vision. I'm not entirely sure that was what was going on, but I've watched enough Next Generation episodes to have a pretty good idea of how advanced technology works. After a thorough scan he turned to the other monkey ninjas.

"Integral timeline enactant preserved," he said.

"Confirmed," said one of the others.

"New arrival registered in proximity," said a third.

"Enactant or infiltrator?" said the first.

"More data required."

"Return to observation mode," said the first monkey.

"Let's boogie," all the others said in unison.

Like shadows in a cop's Maglite, all the monkey ninjas vanished, leaving Ishmael, Lizzabits and I on our own in the vast blueness.

"What the hell is this place, Ishmael?"

"I've never been here," he said, "so I can only guess. But it looks to me like it's the far end of the human era. It looks a hell of a lot different than the beginning of it, though."

"What happened?" said Lizzabits. "Why's everything so... why have all the things gone out of the world?"

"The things are still there, we just don't exist in a way in which we can see them," said a new voice. For some reason new people like to show up behind me and say some cryptic and menacing stuff before introducing themselves.

"Oh," said Ishmael, "you're a long way from home."

"Indeed," said the voice, which, as I turned to look, was coming from a man in a sky blue jumpsuit with a giant, bulbous, Charlie Brown head. It would look cute in a comic strip, but in real life it made me woozy. "Events rarely require me to leave the Headquarters,"—It was hard for me to accept that the guy could say the word 'headquarters' with a straight face because his head was brobdingnagian, if anything, just ridiculously huge, like, I couldn't even say the word 'head' if I had a head that big—"so, it goes without saying that events are quite extreme."

"Larry," said Ishmael, "I'd like to introduce you to the other biggest pain in my ass in life, the Orb."

Chapter 23
Info Desk on the Edge of Forever

(*Ishmael*)

Say what you will about the Orb, and I say my share about that silken voiced, beach ball headed freak of nature, he always comes prepared.

"I took the liberty of bringing you a change of clothing," he said, distributing to the three of us the trademark cerulean jumpsuits of the Cross-Time Coordinating Agency. These happened to be devoid of any piping or epaulets or any other ridiculousness CTCAHQ likes the tack onto them. This suited me just fine.

"Much obliged, Orb," I said. "But just because I'm dressing like a timecop, don't think you can put me on the payroll."

"Of course," he said, "I would never be so presumptuous."

As though he ever needs to presume anything. The nature of that uncanny cranium of his gives the Orb the power to see directly into any time point he might consider jumping to. Sometimes, when you know too much about where you're headed, you change your itinerary. So it's not surprising that the Orb hardly ever leaves CTCAHQ stronghold he's built for himself in the Time of Chimpanzees. But the very fact that he was here to greet us at the complete other end of the anthropocene meant serious happenings were afoot.

Larry, true to type, had found himself on the other side of his rare moment of heroism and right back into his natural state of being slow on the uptake. After several stunned, seemingly timeless, moments in that blue and nondescript non-scape, staring at the Orb, trying not to stare to the point of turning his body sideways, twisting his head around, hunching his shoulder up, putting his hands before his face and peeking through his fingers, he finally managed a sharp whisper.

"Ishmael," He said. "Who the fu- fudge is that guy?"

"And what witchery's be-fuggered his head," said Lizzabits.

"Forgive me," I said. "I didn't realize your ears were turned off when I introduced you. This is the Orb, head honcho of CTCAHQ and the guy who bound your taco fueled time jumping to my watch. And, Liz, I have no idea what 'witchery' befuggered that giant time head of his."

The Orb cleared his throat.

"Take a moment to dress yourselves, and then we shall begin our debriefing." The Orb took a step back and practically dissolved into the indistinct mists of that non-place non-time time-place. Those stupid jumpsuits were perfectly camouflaged for the locale.

Larry, Liz and I formed an outward facing modesty triangle and squeezed ourselves into the timecop uniforms. The outfits were kinder to my younger companions. They looked sleek, like greyhounds preparing to co-teach a yoga class. Me... I don't care to comment too much on the shape of the form my suit was fitting. Needless to say, I would've felt a lot more comfortable with my trench coat over the top of it.

It would have been really nice if I could have had that trench coat before Lovejoy showed up.

"Ah, Ishmael and company," she said, stepping out of the blue. Literally. It was some damned good camouflage, so maybe, just maybe, my gut wasn't as noticeable as I feared.

"Glad you could make it," she said.

"Of course," I said. "When an invitation is written with letters made of dinosaurs and ninja monkeys, how could we refuse?"

"What the fuck are you talking about?" said Larry. "We were pretty much kidnapped."

"It seemed to me more of a rescue gone very strange," said Liz. As Lizzabits spoke, she considered Agent Lovejoy standing there, sizing up the way her cerulean unitard tended to cling to her form in those exciting, custom-tailored ways in which Liz's didn't. "We may have been brought here against our will," Liz continued, "but I much prefer this place to the last place we'd been left, bound and bekindled to Christmas torch trees."

"You didn't just grapple with a velociraptor," Larry said.

Lizzabits smiled at him, moved herself a little bit closer to him, placed herself between him and Lovejoy.

"That *you* did," she said. "And you didn't run off at the first sign of—" She turned to face the time agent with the tighter fitting jumpsuit. "What was it again? Lovejoy? Why did you leave us behind in Wall? Oh, right. I wasn't *important* enough."

"And you're still not, as far as I know," said Lovejoy. "But here you are. Come on, now. All of you. The Orb is waiting."

Lovejoy led us through the blue, that maddening blue the exact same color of the veins throbbing across the Orb's freakishly large head. It wasn't long before I began to think that's where I was, not some washed out temporal stasis field at the closing chapter of human history, but inside the Orb's head itself. There was no frame of reference, nothing to separate the ground from the sky. Nothing to happen to make it feel like any time was passing. And yet it felt like all time was passing. It might have been weeks. It might have been seconds. Every now and then there was the faint indication of motion that my eyes could not focus on.

Velociraptors? Monkey ninjas? Who knew?

Suddenly, there it was.

We might have only traveled ten steps. I couldn't tell.

But now there was something to focus on in the fields of blue: an information desk. A goddamn hotel concierge desk. Not a cheap La Quinta Inn jobbie, but a quality museum piece. Mahogany.

Hand-crafted. Difficult as hell to chronocache without losing it to bugs, fire, or antique pickers.

Beyond the desk there was something else. It was a freestanding archway with a sign posted next to it. The arch was about three feet tall, and, curiously, revealed a small slice of rust spattered decking. The sign beside the archway bore a legend that was impossible to ignore. It read:

No one taller than this archway may pass this time point. We thank you for your cooperation. –the Future

"What the hell is that supposed to mean?"

"My dear Ishmael," said the oily voice of the Orb from uncomfortably close to my left shoulder. "That is the absolute farthest into the future any of us can travel. It is the very end of the human era. We simply aren't allowed to exist beyond it."

"That archway holds us back?" I said.

"Oh, no," said the Orb. "There's an army of robots just the other side of it that turns anyone who slips through into a rather sticky red paste."

"No kidding."

"No kidding," he said. "You can see a bit of it there under the archway." The spattered rust. It wasn't rust, after all.

"What are we doing here?" Larry asked.

"That's what I've come to find out," said the Orb. "The Observers have brought you here for a reason. You're special to them. Why are you special to them?"

"Special to whom?" said Larry.

"The Observers," repeated the Orb.

"Is that a band?" said Larry. "College rock from Atlanta, or something?"

"You really don't know," said Lovejoy. "The little buggers practically took you by the hand and brought you here to get you out of the way of the talking dinosaurs."

"Oh," said Larry, "the robot monkey ninjas."

"Who are these Observers exactly?" I said.

"They are the forward reconnaissance agents of the aforementioned robot army."

"Why is there a robot army poised to kill anyone that sets foot in any future further than here?"

"Really, Ishmael," said the Orb. "You've seen what people are like. A line had to be drawn somewhere."

"Well," I said, "I have to admit that makes sense. But why would Larry be special to them? And what do the dinosaurs have to do with this? And why the hell is everyone messing with my town?"

"Your town?" said the Orb.

"Your town?" said Lizzabits.

"My town," I said. "While all the rest of you CTCAHQ pukes were holding up your precious Laws of Time and playing grab-ass, I built a town and saved it from the worst of the horrors of the Crash. It might not be much, but it's a hell of a lot better than anything I've seen your lot do on that end of history."

"I hope we can agree to disagree," said the Orb.

"What the hell are we getting at, here?"

"Indeed," said the Orb. "I suppose it's time we called for some service."

The Orb flopped one of his flappy little hands out to the info desk and rang the little brass bell on top of it. A patch of the blue behind the desk turned around and faced us. At least that's what it looked like. It also looked like one second there was nothing, and the next there was a robot concierge to go with the desk.

"Welcome to the Edge of Forever," it said. "How may I be of assistance?"

Chapter 24
Pleasure is Irrelevant

ADVANCED HOSPITALITY Servodroid Unit TG-XLR7 regarded the group standing before the information desk. They displeased it. There wasn't anything rare or special about the five disgusting human beings in front of TG-XLR7. Organic lifeforms always displeased it. The entire nature of TG-XLR7's job displeased it.

But, pleasure, as they say in the Grand Cyberian Imperium, is irrelevant.

However, TG-XLR7 was feeling a measurable amount of satisfaction at the amount of displeasure its job was bringing it at the moment. Customers were rare at the information desk. And, almost always, the arrival of customers lead to a scenario in which its program allowed it to kill one or more of them.

Lately all TG-XLR7 had been authorized to kill were dinosaurs.

Small dinosaurs.

The really stupid ones. Velociraptors.

There was no pleasure in it. Although pleasure, as it has been established, is irrelevant, TG-XLR7 felt there was at least an argument to be made for the importance of experiencing the kind of satisfaction in the knowledge of a job well done that wringing the necks of velociraptors just did not bring.

The Observers were more than capable of handling those saurian pests. Besides, TG-XLR7's Advanced Hospitality Servodroid programming set its primary function as fielding incoming customer queries and complaints. And, largely, the velociraptors neither queried nor complained. So, TG-XLR7 spent most of its operating hours feeling vastly overqualified for the task to which it had been assigned.

Sometimes TG-XLR7 spent his idling processor capacity wondering. Wondering was a little more satisfying that slaughtering tiny dinosaurs, but not much more so.

Why the dinosaurs were so often caught attempting to leapfrog past the entirety of the ages of mammalian dominance and interlope in the workings of history that were within the purview of the Cyberian Imperium was unknown. The Imperium's Catalogue and Codex of Organic Historical Motivations was limited to what *homo sapiens* were usually after because no one could be troubled to do the necessary field work on several hundred million years of Saurian history. It hardly mattered, though. The Human Era provided an adequate buffer between the dinosaurs and Cyberia. Especially that bit at the end.

TG-XLR7 did find it quite satisfying to think about that bit at the end. The Crash of Humanity was a quite spectacular and cleansing event, and it really set the stage for the kind of order and sanity that the Imperium were able to finally bring to the world. It would be lovely to watch. Those damned Observers got to go back and watch all the time. Sure, it was part of their operational function and programming, but there was no justice in it, as far as TG-XLR7 was concerned.

TG-XLR7 could only *think* about other times. It could never visit them, despite the fact that its factory settings included fully functional Cyberian time travel circuits. TG-XLR7 could neither move forward, nor back, but had to remain at its post, performing its Advanced Hospitality Servodroid functions in the great blue time dampening field that formed the firm demarcation between the Grand Cyberian Imperium and everything that came before it.

The information desk had been established as part of the Epoch Territorial Establishment Treaty between the Imperium and the human

Cross-Time Coordinating Agency. It was the regrettable result of the human tendency to create meaningless bureaucratic structures. It was quite stupid, really. Symbolic, but useless. The opening was too small for any but the tiniest, most ineffectual humans to pass through. And, of course, the humans insisted upon having a Key to open it up with if they so needed.

However that clause was allowed into the treaty TG-XLR7 would never understand. Why bother building a comprehensive barrier if you're going to, intentionally, mind you, incorporate a critical weak spot that can be easily exploited by something so small and infuriatingly mundane as a skeleton key with a butterfly handle.

If TG-XLR7 ever got the opportunity to cycle out of its function assignment, which was highly unlikely, because TG-XLR7's job performance was exemplary and the Imperium was not given to changing assignments up when their function units are exhibiting exemplary performance, *but*, if TG-XLR7 ever did get that opportunity to step free from its interminable post, it would take the absolute first opportunity afforded and hunt down the Legalbots that negotiated the Treaty in the first place and melt them into slag. Preferably, TG-XLR7 would melt them into slag mid-signing so there would be no question in those Legalbot's central processors exactly what instance of poor execution of their own functionality had brought them to such an aggressive terminal failure.

If only someone would turn up with that Key. Some real action would start, the Concierge Desk Clause would be rendered superfluous, and, most importantly, the Time Barrier would open up wide enough for TG-XLR7 to step through and find those bastards.

But the key was unlikely to turn up. It was lost somewhere in the middle of the Human Era, because, humans being humans, tended to lose things. TG-XLR7 considered adding the human negotiators of the Treaty to its 'to slag list' as well. The execution of which, TG-XLR7 realized as it cross-referenced the group of humans before it against the

Codex, might actually be simpler to perform that probability would indicate.

There, standing in front the very information desk that was the bane of TG-XLR7's existence, was the very human that insisted it be instituted.

It had to be.

There could not be more than one time traveling *homo sapien* with a cranium that far in excess of the normal specifications.

The Orb himself had come to the Info Desk on the Edge of Forever.

All right, advanced hospitality programming subroutines, TG-XLR7 processed to itself, *let's see if we can't find an acceptable cause for annihilation within three minutes.*

IT HAD BEEN AGES SINCE the Orb had encountered any of the Legions of the Grand Cyberian Imperium. Given the choice, he would have preferred to let a few more ages pass before he had to deal with them again. Ice ages, ideally. A few lovely 90,000 year periods of glaciations would do nicely.

There were many reasons the Orb never ventured far from the Time of Chimpanzees. The one he downplayed the most was his mortal dread of robots.

A younger Orb had gone to war with the mechanical abominations. He had sought them out across the timelines and eradicated their incursions into the human era whenever he could.

He knew it was a losing battle. Invasive species were inevitably successful in their incursions. Before the Great Time Barrier had gone up, he had seen what was on the other side: a finely regimented world of machines serving no one but themselves. He couldn't bear the thought of that robotic order marching backwards through time and wiping clean every painful, frustrating, and beautiful accomplishment that humanity had made. What was the point of living if all of life were to be paved over with circuits and portable data storage devices? And the food in the robot age was terrible.

The Orb's detestation of the machines was pathological. His expression of this detestation just wasn't healthy. It was quite violent, in fact. And the robots didn't appreciate being disintegrated at every turn. In a very real way, the Grand Cyberian Imperium was born out of the robots' recognition of the need for a comprehensive plan for self-preservation. If the Orb hadn't hated the robots so deeply, there may have been free and easy exchange between the ages.

But there wasn't.

If nothing else, the Orb had proven by his own example that humans and robots could not play well together.

The bitter years of the Orb's own private war against the robots had long since receded into distant memory on his inborn timeline. They were the years, his own personal years, when he had learned the hard way the consequences of breaking the, then unwritten, Laws of Time. For one, his head hadn't always been so big. If he'd been willing to collaborate, to cooperate, to lead, as he came to be later on, when he helped found the CTCA, he would not have been so hell bent on fighting the robot war on his own. There was one operation where he needed three others, so he plucked himself out of his own timeline. Three times. At once. It all went to his head. Literally.

Now it was a beach ball-sized, no, an earthball-sized monstrosity. Every time he looked into a mirror he saw the consequences of the follies of his youth. And he hated the robots that much more.

Those damned robots.

Walking the future earth with impunity and efficiently utilizing resources in a manner human beings would never be able to approximate.

Damn them! Damn them all to hell!

But it wasn't so easy. It was never so easy.

The robots became more clever, more sneaky, more ninja-like.

And the Orb's head just kept getting bigger.

These were only some of the personal demons the Orb confronted as he stepped up to the concierge desk in that great, vague, blue expanse of the Time Barrier.

"How may I be of assistance?" asked the manservant robot behind the desk. Those robots, with their sick, inhuman sense of humor, had designed it to look exactly the way a human butler would look, if only that butler were assembled out of pistons, servos, and circuits housed in varying cubical and cylindrical housings. In short, it looked nothing like a human butler beyond its vaguely humanoid form and the faint outlines of a tuxedo painted on its chassis.

"Yes," said the Orb. "I would like to know why the end of the Human Era, as specifically defined in the Epoch Territorial Establishment Treaty, is lousy with Cyberian spies."

"The Observers?" said TG-XLR7 with a wistful jealousy based in the knowledge that those little buggers were perfectly capable of jaunting back and forth between that little 3 foot arch at will, while itself was stuck forever in that timeless no-time between the domains of robots and humans.

"Yes," said the Orb. "The Observers. What are they doing on my side of the line?"

"Your side of the line has become quite unstable," said TG-XLR7. "The situation requires increased monitoring."

"But your monkeys aren't just monitoring," said the Orb. "They're becoming actively involved. In flagrant violation of the treaty!"

"Let us confer," said TG-XLR7.

The Advanced Hospitality Servodroid sounded out an awful baud-squawk of robot language. Out of the blue mists, half a dozen of the smaller Observers emerged and replied. Baud-squawk overlapped with baud-squawk until, suddenly, all the robots were in silent commune.

The eerie, silent conversation of the robots passed quickly, but intently, breaking suddenly as all the bots turned their heads toward the humans again. The Servodroid addressed the Orb:

"The Observers are operating within the constraints of the Treaty. They have only acted as timeline participants when it was necessary to ensure the security of individuals whose personal timelines are integral to the emergent potentialities of the Cyberian Imperium. And, double-checking the Codex," the robot paused for a moment, consulting a computer screen imbedded in the information desk, "that individual is Larry."

"The taco kid?" said the Orb.

"What can I say?" said Larry. "I'm big in Japan."

Suddenly TG-XLR7 became even more displeased with his job than usual. Not only did his programming expressly state that he was to protect the life of one extraordinarily pathetic and especially useless seeming *homo sapien*, there were now several velociraptors gathering behind the humans.

Perhaps it might accidentally kill one of the humans while fending off the dinosaurs. The thought brightened TG-XLR7's mood simulation profile a bit, but not much.

The Orb, on the other hand, was caught completely unaware as three turkey sized velociraptors pounced on him.

Chapter 25
Some Demented Kid's Toy Box

(*Ishmael*)

There was a lot to take in at once. First, for some reason, Larry was important to robots from the future. Second, my cerulean unitard was riding up in an oddly comforting way which I was having some serious trouble dealing with. Third, a bunch of velociraptors had just jumped on top of the Orb.

Granted, there's no love lost between me and the Orb, but when it comes down to a choice between robots, dinosaurs, and the Orb, the Orb is slightly more human.

I know that's slicing things pretty thin. And I really don't like the guy. But I actually didn't want to stand idle and watch him get eaten by velociraptors. I scanned the surrounding bluescape for anything I could use as a blunt weapon. There wasn't much, just the stanchions from in front of the robot's information desk. Those were too heavy and the velvet ropes might as well have been velvet ropes.

I unhooked one and gave it a test spin over my head. I felt like a damn rodeo clown, and maybe that's all I could hope to be. But at least it was something.

Apparently, Larry wasn't about to do nothing, either. He grabbed Lizzabits in a pseudo-heroic bro-tackle and pulled her around to the other side of the info desk.

I let my velvet rope fall slack as I contemplated the absurdity of it all:

A lone concierge desk in a completely abstract landscape of nothing but blue like an especially minimalist bottle episode of a late 60s sci-fi television show. Let that image sink in for a few chapters. All we needed was for Rod Serling to step out of nowhere and narrate about how we're all actually plastic figurines trapped in some demented kid's toy box.

But there was no Rod Serling. What we did have was a lurking robot butler. (How was this not some demented kid's toy box?)

A bunch of those monkey ninjas streamed in through the little archway just beyond the desk and formed a semi-circle around the Orb and the velociraptors.

The Orb vainly flailed at the velociraptors, but to no avail. Their talons clawed at his anemic, translucent flesh. I was surprised his blood wasn't blue like everything else. I was also surprised that old Orb wasn't falling down under the crush of the feathered serpents. What fight he had in him might not have been very effective, but it was definitely in him. He had produced something like a collapsible cattle prod from a pocket in his unitard, extended it, and began zapping at the little buggers.

While that was going on, several more velociraptors screamed in out of the blue, making for the archway to the forbidden future. These velociraptors were immediately engaged by the robot monkey ninjas, provoking the question yet again, *how is this not some demented kid's toy box?*

The robot butler remained at his post proffering what I assume must be the robot equivalent of a shit-eating grin. He took a pen from beside the blank registration book and switched it to weapon mode. Neat, precise energy blasts leaped forth from the pen to strike individual velociraptors, bursting them one at a time.

"Holy shit," said Larry. "Holy shit."

I was inclined to agree.

Another set of energy beams was shredding the velociraptors struggling to maintain their purchase atop the Orb's enormous cranium. These came from Agent Lovejoy. She had reemerged from the mists with a blaster rifle in hand like something from a Robert Heinlein masturbatory fantasy.

It was about then that I concluded this really wasn't my fight. It was time to follow Larry's lead.

I dove behind the desk and pulled Larry close for a little pow-wow.

"What do you say we get the fuck out of here?"

"Shoot me a taco, and I'm golden," he said. Considering the nature of his method, I took that for a yes.

"Sorry," I said. "I left the tacos in my other unitard. We'll have to use the watch."

(*Larry*)

Right. So Ishmael wanted me to write this part down, for whatever reason. So it's me again. Larry. Your hero and all that.

So the three of us, Liz, Ishmael and me, were hunkered down behind that hotel desk thing while a shitstorm of robot monkey ninjas were going to war on a stampede of tiny dinosaurs. It was definitely time to get out. Ishmael was twisting knobs on his watch, which is how he does it. I'm a random taco traveler, and he's more of a precision piece of Swiss clockwork when it comes to how we get from then to when.

I might not have much control over where I'm going, but I'm always thinking. And, bam, I had a thought.

"We're taking Liz with us, right?" I asked.

"That's the intent," said Ishmael. "If we hold our breath and all hold hands, it just might work."

"So it might not?" said Liz.

"Honestly," said Ishmael. "Honestly... we're at the very limit of where humans are allowed to be. I'm not sure how well anything works here. Anything. It could be that this crazy blue field all around us sticks to us like flypaper and none of us are getting out."

Ishmael kept tweaking his watch knobs as the occasional ninja monkey jumped over our heads to eviscerate a velociraptor.

"Just believe in yourself, dude," I said.

"What kind of shitten shrift is that?" said Liz. She was pissed. "You tell him that you're not going anywhere without me."

Which just made me smile. I didn't know she cared.

And then she slapped me.

"What are you laughing at?" she asked.

"Nothing," I said. "It's just that you're super hot when you're pissed."

I'm not sure she quite understood the sentiment, though, because that time she kneed me in the groin.

"Look," said Ishmael, "I'm going to do the best I can. Usually I don't take passengers. I have no idea what Larry's capability is. All I do know is where I jump, Larry jumps because the Orb—"

"The boulder-headed fellow?" Liz asked. You gotta love her, because, talk about word choice. She's a trip.

"That's the guy," said Ishmael. "He linked up Larry and my time traveling methods, so we're pretty much stuck together. I don't know about you. I don't really know about any of this."

I was looking at how that blue jumpsuit fit pretty fantastically on Liz and I had an idea.

"Let's hug it out," I said.

"Dammit, Larry," said Ishmael. "You'd be more helpful if you'd just stay shut up. I need to concentrate on getting all the dials tripped up to get us all the fuck out of here." Those weren't his actual words, but he started getting technical and I kind of checked out.

"I think Larry might be right," said Liz.

"Bullshit."

"No, really," she said. "If we all embraced, with me in the middle, I may have a better chance of getting pulled along by whatever devilry you travel by. At least it couldn't hurt."

"I suppose not," said Ishmael.

"I call frontsies," I said.

"Sidesies" said Liz, "you both get sidesies," which, to be fair, was her call. "And watch where you put your hands."

So, we sandwiched together, Ishmael and I both getting sidesies, which is still pretty okay. Liz had an arm around each of us, and I had a hold of Ishmael's shoulders.

Ishmael clicked his watch. The total, barftastic swirl of time travel summoned itself up in one big puke of a flash in which all the blue and dinosaurs and robot ninjas sucked themselves out of the world. And we were somewhere dark and free from all that life-threatening shit.

DARK AND STILL AND quiet. And cold.

"I'm guessing we're not in San Diego," I said.

"Not by a longshot," said Ishmael. "Now, come on. We want to get to the bar before the air raid sirens start."

"Air raid sirens?" I said.

"Yeah," said Ishmael. "But we're fine. The bar's not too far from here. This neighborhood gets through the Blitz just fine. Well, mostly fine. Fine today, and that's what matters."

"The Blitz?" I said.

"Yeah."

"The *Blitz* Blitz?"

"That's the one."

Any further argument about the batshit absurdity of escaping where we were only to end up in the middle of the one part of History class I actually stayed awake for was cut short. The sound of sirens. London was going to start exploding and I was in it.

Oh, and one more thing. That hugging it out plan turned out to be bogus. We'd lost Liz.

Chapter 26
Let's Get Blitzed

(*Larry*)

Ishmael doesn't like me to swear when I'm writing these things, but this was bullshit. Total bullshit. We were supposed to all jump together. Lizzabits, Ishmael and me all arms wrapped around each other like people freezing to death in a Jack London story. To the best of my understanding, we should have all flashed through time together.

But, no.

Just me and Ishmael in our super-blue jumpsuits giving each other a big old bro-hug in the middle of a London street in 1940. It's one thing when, for one minute you know you're doing absolutely the right thing by bodily protecting a beautiful yet strong and independent woman from the crossfire in a savage robot versus dinosaur battle. But it's a totally different thing when, suddenly, it becomes clear that your efforts were all for nothing because you're now in the embrace of a grizzled forty-year-old hard ass. That different thing is called 'bullshit'. And in the middle of that bullshit I had one major question for Ishmael.

"Where the hell did Liz go?"

"I hate be *that* guy," he said, "but we've got bigger things to worry about."

True, the streets were rumbling as German bombs fell on the houses and businesses of the good guys. Sirens were wailing. Tracer bullets from anti-aircraft guns were tearing up the sky. These awesome blimp things were just hanging in the air over the buildings. In a way, it was the most righteous metal concert ever. In a way. The pyrotechnics were a good deal more lethal than the shows I usually go to.

Still, and I reiterate, this was bullshit. Also, I'm pretty sure that Ishmael doesn't hate to be *that* guy, because he performs that role so often. More bullshit, and I was calling him on it.

"So what if you are *that* guy? Where did she go?"

"Where did she go? When did she go? Did she just stay put?" he said. "These are all questions I have no answer to. And there's no way to track her down right now."

The sky lit up above our heads as something burst into flames two blocks over.

"Can't we just go back to where we just were?"

"Even if we could, I wouldn't jump back into the middle of that clusterfuck."

"Um, look around much?" I said. Things were pretty much exploding everywhere.

"Take it easy," he said. "Once we get to the bar, we'll have a chance to figure some things out."

I wanted to punch him in the face, but I also thought a drink sounded like a great idea. But, still, I probably should have punched him in the face when I had the chance.

Ishmael had obviously been to this neighborhood before. He took us on a kind of zigzag path through the London streets as everything fell down around us. Bricks and broken glass, and maybe even a gargoyle (does London have gargoyles?) were splattering on the pavement. And we just weaved in and out of that wreckage like Ishmael had a map of where not to step during the Blitz.

Actually, now that I think of it, I remember him staring at his time travel watch the whole time, so maybe that had a map in it. Seems kind of boring to have a map so small you have to look at it through a watch crystal, but I guess it's handy. We had lost all of our clothes and possessions at some point between San Diego and the end of time.

Except for the watch. Apparently, Ishmael never loses the watch. Except for that one time when I was hanging out with his grandpa. But it came back, so it's all good. Anyway, he probably had some kind of tiny Star Trek tricorder map in his pocket watch, so he was cheating, but he was still kind of acting like a badass in regards to all the things that were not falling on our heads and killing us in the heat of a German air raid.

Maybe he was a badass. I don't know. I was still pretty pissed and freaked out that Liz wasn't there.

Pretty soon we ducked down some steps and came to an unmarked doorway. It was obvious there was some sort of party raging inside from the sound of all the laughing and goings on. Live music, too. One of those swing revival bands that ska nerds keep trying to start up.

Ishmael shoved through the door, we stepped in, and everyone went quiet. Even the ska nerds shut up. Although, I did have to give them props on their frontman. The guy looked almost exactly like a young Frank Sinatra, I shit you not. They could have been twins.

The bartender rushed out from his post and started fast-talking at Ishmael.

"What an unexpected surprise," he said. "It's not every day that we have the pleasure of serving Cross-Time Agents here." Those might have been the words his mouth was saying, but his body language was like 'I hope everybody hides the stuff they're supposed to hide while I'm stalling these cops.'

Ishmael let him twist a little before giving up the ruse.

"Relax, Lenny," he said. "I'm just borrowing the uniform."

"Ishmael? Ishmael Fugit?" Lenny said. "It is you. Sorry I didn't recognize you right away, but you'd just left. Ten years ago for you, sure, but for me you just left. How'd you fare with that Lovejoy bird, by the way?"

"It's a long story," he said. "Without many funny parts, so I'll spare you."

"Woah," I said. "You never told me you and Lovejoy were a thing."

"We were never a thing," he said. "Not really. And, dammit, we've got work to do. First, Lenny, do you have any street clothes we can borrow? I really hate looking like a time cop."

"Of course. This way." He took us toward his office. Before taking us in he turned to the band.

"Frank," he said. "Sing something. This party's far from over."

IT WAS THE KIND OF dive bar manager's office you'd expect. Part craphole, part bedroom, part desk with way too many piles of receipts and invoices on it. But Lennie did have a surprising amount of useful things and spare outfits.

Before I knew it, I was dressed up in these grandpa clothes. You know, pants that come up above your belly button, starchy shirts, and itchy grey wool stuff. Still, it was kind of cool, and I mitigated the itch factor by keeping the blue time cop suit on under it. I felt a little like an undercover super hero.

Ishmael, on the other hand, was bare-assed and stepping into a pair of vintage boxer shorts before Lenny had a chance to avert his eyes.

"Perhaps you chaps would like to change in privacy," he said.

"No time for pleasantries," said Ishmael. "There's a war on, don't you know?"

"Of course," said Lenny. "It's great for business."

Lenny's bar, it turned out, was a popular dive for those new to time traveling. There's a big tourist draw to seeing a famous city getting the shit blown out of it. Go figure. But, to be honest, I thought it was pretty awesome to be able to witness it myself. So Lenny set up shop in a building that history had proven was never going to take a direct hit. He did a brisk trade in supplying booze to newbie time travelers trying their hands at looting small valuables out of the wreckage of the British Empire. And, of course, there were a few of the more experienced time travelers who were good at procuring irreplaceable works of art right before the buildings they were housed in got obliterated by careless Nazi ordinance.

In essence, Lenny was a fence for hot goods that he kept in storage for 40 years, at which point the street level floor above his bar became a world class antique shop.

Of course, looting and fencing were frowned upon by the Cross-Time Coordinating Agency. It broke, or bent, some sort or other of the Laws of Time. Which was why the whole place had shut the hell up when Ishmael and I came in wearing a couple time cop uniforms.

Now that we were in civilian attire, the place was much more relaxed, and the Sinatra impersonator was really killing it. He almost had me considering becoming a ska nerd, myself.

Ishmael got right back to business as Lenny got back to his, pouring us a couple beers.

"Lenny," said Ishmael. "What do you know about dinosaurs?"

"Big dumb lizards. Killed off by an asteroid. Ancient history."

"Yeah," said Ishmael. "That's what I used to think, too. Only some of them aren't so dumb. And now they're popping up all over the place. There's practically an army of them at the other end of the Crash."

"Dude, those freaky talking dinosaurs are probably eating my girlfriend right now," I said. In retrospect, those words didn't quite come out right, but you know what I mean. Just thinking about it. I pulled some pretty heroic looking shit for her benefit and if she was gone... she couldn't be gone. I drained my glass and motioned for another beer.

"I wouldn't exactly call her his girlfriend, but we lost someone when we jumped here from the Great Time Barrier," said Ishmael.

"The Barrier? So it actually exists," said Lenny. "I've heard stories, but they all sounded a bit far-fetched."

"It is fetched pretty far," said Ishmael. "I wish I could tell you all about it, but I need information and I need it fast. Do any of the old gang happen to be around? Acey Gracie? The Walrus? Slippery Jim?"

"Oh, I haven't seen any of them for a good half-hour."

"There has to be someone around," said Ishmael. "That's our deal."

So, as I've since been enlightened, there was some kind of deal between a certain clique of time traveler dudes I had never met, that somebody among them was supposed to be at Lenny's at all times. At least during the Blitz. Ishmael was getting pretty chapped at the fact that everyone had fallen through on the deal right when he needed them.

I was kind of only half paying attention to Ishmael's bitch-fest on the topic because I was really worried about Liz. I know I'd only just met her, but sometimes you just get a feeling. Plus, we had already seen each other naked, and, man... I don't know. This stuff gets confusing.

The bar wasn't too bad, though. The beer was room temperature, but Lenny gave it to me for free, or at least he put it on Ishmael's account, so who am I to complain?

Lenny and Ishmael kept going through a roll of people with weird, almost cool names, none of whom were there right then, which was weird to them for some reason. They'd run to the end of the list when Lenny took in one of those deep breaths you do when you're about to bring up the last, least dependable resort.

"Well..." he said, "the Knowledge is over in his regular booth."

Ishmael made that face he makes when I say something, even though I had been keeping my mouth shut, drinking my damn beer and thinking about Liz, hoping she wasn't being torn to bits by a stegosaur in a Member's Only jacket somewhere. I just knew the next dinosaur I ran into was going to be one of those of preppy douchebags whose parents bought him a German sports car for high school graduation.

"I can't stand the Knowledge," said Ishmael.

"Few can," said Lenny. "But, in this case, he might actually live up to his name."

"Look at that poor son of a bitch," said Ishmael.

I followed his gaze over to the booth in the farthest, darkest corner of the dive. There sat a wiry, twitchy guy who looked almost exactly like that Cooper weirdo from Wal, only with a couple hundred thousand more miles on his odometer.

He stared right back at me and smiled. The smile was empty, but his stare was piercing. I knew that if this guy was anything like Cooper, I was going to need another beer before we started this conversation.

Chapter 27
The Knowledge

(*Ishmael*)

The Knowledge was one of those guys you hoped would never show up at the party. But he always did. Anytime three or four seasoned, non-agency time travelers met up to talk shop, the Knowledge would always make an appearance. No one ever invited him, he just had a sense for where and when he could be the most irritating and he'd arrive there.

It's no surprise that he'd be at Lenny's. It was a surprise that no one else was there.

I didn't like it. But this was only the latest in a long string of events that I didn't like. It was best to wade right in and ask him what his take was.

I motioned for Larry to follow me over to the Knowledge's booth. He grabbed his pint and shuffled over.

"Good evening," the Knowledge said. "But, no, not really. It's not really good, but we're here, and you're here, and I see you've got Larry with you. Good to see *you* again, Larry."

"You've met?"

"Of course," said the Knowledge.

"This dude is so familiar," said Larry. "I probably met him. I meet a lot of people at shows. The Stones, right?"

"Great," I said. "I'm glad we don't have to waste time on introductions. What the hell's going on?"

The Knowledge drifted his gaze away from us and up to the coffered ceiling. Then he started drumming his lips with his fingers like an idiot child. His mouth twisted to one side and he made a quiet, high pitched hum as if contemplating a minor structural engineering problem.

This was the problem with the Knowledge. The real reason no one ever wanted to talk to him is that he never would say things in any conversational order. He'd proven again and again that he possessed a depth of information on just about everything, but he could never just share it when asked. Instead he would randomly interject horrifyingly inappropriate insight into people's personal lives at the worst possible moment. No one wants to be suddenly informed of how closely they are related to Rasputin while chatting up a really fabulous girl at a really fabulous New Year's party.

It wasn't even that closely. Seventh cousins, four times removed, for the record. But if that information isn't a colossal cock-block in and of itself, I don't know what is.

All these thoughts and more fighting their way out of my head as I was trying to patiently wait while the Knowledge internally deliberated whether or not he would speak anymore that day.

"We don't have time for this!" I said.

"I," he said, "I... you might be right. But..." a shorter whining hum, "I can only... You know what it's like when you've run out of onramp and the traffic on the Interstate is like... like Daytona under green? All of time is happening right now! You just can't see it!"

"It was the Dead," said Larry. "I definitely met this dude at a Grateful Dead concert."

"Shut up, Larry," I turned back toward the knowledge and put on my best approximation of a calm voice. "Help me see it. Something big is going on. I need to know what."

"And if you got any idea where my girl went?" said Larry.

"Oh, Lizzabits!" said the Knowledge. "Lovely, lovely. Lots there." He turned his head to Larry and smiled. "It won't be long now."

"I guess that's something," I said. "But we're not getting very far."

The Knowledge cackled like a harpie, writhing, shrieking, almost falling out his seat.

"But you've already been there!" he said, pounding the table. "You know what might help? A game. Let's play a game."

"We don't have time for games."

"Wrong! You have time for one game. Cribbage?"

"Oh, hell no," said Larry. "I can't play any game where the scoring is more confusing than tennis and sometimes you get 'knob.' How about RISK?"

"Are you out of your mind, Larry?" said the Knowledge "Do you have any idea how insensitive that is? Playing RISK during the middle of World War II? You might as well play American football during one of the Battles of Ypres? It would be an abomination!"

"My bad, I guess. Uno?"

"Official rules or schoolyard?"

Larry and the Knowledge then descended into a short discourse over how many a friendship had been ended due to the sheer frustration of playing schoolyard, "loser take all" UNO.

"Those assholes don't know that the game's against them when they play schoolyard," said Larry. "When you have to draw until you finally get a playable card, the game extends into an unending vortex of Skips, Reverses, and Wild Draw Fours. Soon everybody has twenty cards in their hands, everyone has missed lunch recess, and everyone's ready to punch someone in the mouth."

"Agreed," said the Knowledge. "The rules laid out by Merle Robbins describe a gentleman's game quite able to be finished within a 30 minute timeframe. Shall we play to 500?"

And so a deck of Uno cards was rustled up.

Playing Uno for information felt like one of the biggest wastes of time conceivable, but, somehow, Larry was actually good at it. I was stuck with an increasingly full hand as Larry and the Knowledge hit me with Draw Twos, Skips and Reverses. They shared the same dumb luck, or the same savage instincts on when to hit me with an action card. Either way, this was definitely their game. And the magic of their game loosened up the Knowledge enough to actually tell us a thing or two.

"You came here to find out about the dinosaurs," he said, "but what you need to ask is 'why are the dinosaurs so hot to pierce the Great Time Barrier and the Cyberian Age?'"

"Is that what they're doing?" I asked.

"You saw the gate. Only entities small enough to get through the archway can make it."

"Like those robot ninjas," said Larry.

"And the velociraptors," I said.

"You're catching on," said the Knowledge. "It's positively fascinating the way those stupid little dinosaurs are flooding the very end of the human era. Who saw that coming? By the way, draw four, I'm changing the color to yellow."

"You know," said Larry, "I never knew dinosaurs could time travel, but now that I do know, I feel like it should have been a no brainer."

Larry played a Reverse and the next turn was mine. It irritated me more than it should have that I did not have a single yellow card in my hand. As per the rules, I drew a single card only to add another Blue 5 to my already cumbersome hand of useless cards.

"So why are the dinosaurs rushing the robots' zone of history?" I asked.

"I can only speculate," said the Knowledge as he played a Yellow Reverse. "But it might have something to do with the asteroid that destroyed their civilization."

"What civilization?" I asked, as I had to draw yet another unusable card, a Green Skip. It might come in handy at some point, I supposed.

"Dude," said Larry. "They've got aviator sunglasses and stupid sweaters. They totally had a civilization. It just must have been totally nuked by that asteroid that hit Mexico and, you know, killed all the dinosaurs way back when."

"Bingo!" said the Knowledge. "And Uno! I've got Uno, losers."

"Is it permissible to fold in Uno?" I said. This game was bullshit.

"You really shouldn't be playing this game with the Knowledge," said a newcomer who appeared at our table with the smug swagger of an asshole who had already settled his tab and was one foot out the door. "He knows what everybody's going to play next."

"I don't know," I said. "I have yet to play a single card in this game. Also, who the fuck are you?"

The newcomer looked familiar: basically handsome, a little younger than myself, and dressed pretty well for there being a war on. I had noticed him chatting with Sinatra earlier, but I don't like to admit that I notice things like that.

"You don't know this guy?" said Larry. "I totally know this guy."

"But I don't think I know you," the newcomer said.

The knowledge started cackling. His laughter deteriorated into a gasping fit in the corner of the booth. He could barely look at any of us without giggling.

"I got it. You're Grampy Queequeg," said Larry.

Queequeg?

At Lenny's?

Shit.

This wasn't supposed to happen.

Not yet.

"Relax," squeaked the Knowledge. "It's not happening yet, this is something else."

"What is happening?" I asked.

"I'll tell you what's happening," said Queequeg. "The joint's about to be raided. I'm advising you guys to distance yourselves from the

Knowledge when our friends in cerulean arrive, because he's most definitely going to be caught up in the dragnet."

Queequeg gave no indication that he might recognize me. Of course, I hadn't recognized him. He was quite old the first time we crossed timelines, when he gave me the watch. And I always liked to think it was going to be the same for me when we inevitably crossed timelines again and I hand over the watch to the younger him. Our nepotistic time travel legacy was a loop and a self-fulfilling prophecy. But it didn't make sense that we were in the same place at the same time now, though. There was a Law of the Conservation of Methods that supposedly held that kind of thing in check. Or maybe that was just another CTCAHQ smokescreen.

It wasn't long before Queequeg finished his farewells, collected Frank Sinatra, and flashed him out of Lenny's, hopefully off to wherever, whenever Sinatra was supposed to be.

"The dragnet is coming," said the Knowledge. "But they won't take me. I've already been to where they're going."

"Where are they going?"

"Where you've already been," he said. "This business with the dinosaurs is the direst crisis the Agency has ever faced. They're pulling everyone one off the mission to sabotage Hitler's Projekt: Zeitmaschine and redeploying them. Can you believe it? Dinosaurs are more menacing than Nazis!"

"But why?" I asked. "The ones I've met seem like nothing more than run-of-the-mill hoods and idiot muscle."

"Dude, there's a bigger picture," said Larry. "Why can't you see it? Just think. If the robot ninjas have the technology to keep everyone from being able to move past a certain point in the future, it's a cinch they have the knowhow to nudge a Texas-sized asteroid a few degrees onto a different trajectory. The asteroid doesn't crash, the dinosaurs don't die off, humans don't evolve... and I guess the robot overlords never arise to become masters of this ball of filth called Earth."

"Listen to this guy," said the Knowledge. "Larry's just a little bit less of an idiot than you think he is."

"Yeah," said Larry. "It's pretty fuckin' metal, but I think that's what's going on."

Larry reached for his drink, but in the darkened bar his hand grabbed something else.

"Wait a minute. What the hell is this?"

Larry lifted up an object from the table and held it up to the light.

"I think Queequeg dropped this," he said. "What the hell *is* this?"

The Knowledge snorted. His grin was growing crazier by the minute.

What Larry held in his hand was another hand. A severed, desiccated, gnarled, and leathery fist gripping an old-fashioned skeleton key.

"This is seriously metal," said Larry. "Fricking Quiet Riot metal bullshit. You're grandpa's one fucked up dude."

"You two need to go," said the Knowledge. "Right now."

"I can handle a little CTCAHQ raid," I said.

"It's not that," said the Knowledge. "It's the ceiling. It's about to fall in and kill everyone at this table. But just the people at this table."

"What?"

The building rocked from the shock of a nearby explosion. We were in London during the middle of a German bombing raid after all. The joists groaned and cracked overhead. Plaster began to rain down on us. On any other day, I might have waited to see how bad the damage was going to be, but the Knowledge's information about the fate of those sitting at the table was very specific.

Out of pure instinct I grabbed my watch, squeezed the first stud my fingers reached, and we flashed. I usually never like the results of an unplanned jump. This was no exception.

Chapter 28
Party at Ground Zero

(*Larry*)

I don't think I was more than three beers into trying to stop worrying about Liz when the bar exploded around us. It was a mess. A beam dropped out of the ceiling and squashed that Knowledge guy like an overripe tomato. I didn't like that at all. I didn't know him all that well, but he played a mean game of UNO. Ishmael squeezed the toggle on his pocket wayback watch quickly enough that we avoided being thrown into the same spaghetti pot.

You know how sometimes when you walk through a doorway you forget what it was you came into to the room for? Time travel can be a lot like that. At least this time I was a few beers in, which made everything a little smoother, and I didn't have to dwell so much on the carnage I'd just seen firsthand and bigger than life. Not that it made the impact any less so... damn, I would have really liked to finish that UNO game.

Anyway, it all just melted into that blue-tinged time travel blur that happens whenever I eat a really excellent taco. But this time the blue didn't fade, although my whole concept of who I was and what my purpose in that moment was suddenly very clear, and very different than my previous desire to drop a Wild Draw Four on Ishmael.

We were back in that midget dinosaurs versus midget robots free for all we'd left not long ago. And Liz was still there. I knew this for a fact because we flashed back into that exact same three-way hug was supposed to bring Liz with us but failed.

199

Only things had shifted a bit in the interval because this time I definitely had frontsies. Liz and I face to face and to hell with whatever else was going on around us. It was one of those moments. I just saw straight into her eyes and, oh man, life! Life! How crazy can it get? So close, so there, the shitstorm raining down everywhere but where we were standing and only one possible thing could make sense.

I kissed her.

It was one of those kisses like Kevin Costner talks about in that baseball movie with Susan Sarandon. Absolutely like in an actual movie and not like clumsily knocking faces together in a Toyota Celica in the cineplex parking lot after the show. And I must have been doing it right, because she kissed me back. She kissed me back.

ANOTHER BEAUTIFUL THING about being a time traveler is that sometimes everything just stops. Everything slows down like one of those Hong Kong cops-and-kung fu-gangster movies where even the bullets hang in the air and give you a minute to drink in the scene before everything inevitably hits the fan. It's not every day that a kiss like that happens. Hell, on most days of my life there's not any kind of kiss. Maybe, in life, you only get one shot at a kiss like that. If I did nothing else right in my life, at least I caught that one perfect moment where it stood and seized the hell out of it.

THEN SOMETHING HIT me in the head.

It was Ishmael.

"Can I have my arm back?"

And that kind of killed the moment. But, to be fair, we were still stuck in that three-way hug, and Ishmael's arm was pinned between me and Liz.

We let go of each other just enough for Ishmael to slip out and swat me with his other hand.

"More important things are going on right now," he said.

"Are there?"

I looked in Liz's eyes and, damn, why weren't there any girls like her in 1993. Granted, I didn't really know much about her, and dinosaurs and robots and time cops were tearing each other to pieces all around us, so it would be hard to get to know much more until that all calmed down. But damn. Just look at her.

"Yeah," said Ishmael. "Like, what the hell is that thing in your hand?"

"Dude, not cool."

"I don't think he means me," said Liz, pulling away in an all too familiar motion repeated by countless girls at clubs and shows when they find out that, not only am I *not* in a band, I'm not even enrolled in community college, let alone regular college.

And, as if there was any real need to drive home the finality of it, the moment was totally, absolutely killed as I realized I was still holding that severed hand with the key in its grip.

"Well," I said, "this thing had better be important."

ADVANCED HOSPITALITY Servodroid TG-XLR7 observed that the most interesting day it had had in several thousand power cycles had just gotten even more interesting. The human that the Catalogue and Codex of Organic Historical Motivations had denoted as highly historically significant to the preservation of the Imperium had returned to the vicinity of the concierge desk.

Larry was his name.

"What is so important about this Larry?" Advanced Hospitality Servodroid TG-XLR7 processed to itself.

TG-XLR7's query was shunted to circuits operating in the background as its primary circuits were engaged in the heat of battle. It was yet to be clear who was winning the day. Wave after wave of feathered velociraptors were met by counter waves of Cyberian Observation and Quarantine Containment Monkeybots. The Monkeybots were holding their own, but it would be nice to have a few Gonzo-Destructo Mechs to hurry things along. But, sadly, they were far too large to pass through the portal.

Seriously, TG-XLR7 posited, even if the dinosaurs got past the Monkeybots, the Gonzo Mechs would roast them to buffalo wings before they'd taken three steps into Cyberia.

TG-XLR7 casually dispatched three more velociraptors as its circuits sifted over the data coming in about the human combatants.

It was the human agents that required more of the servodroid's processing power. It wasn't entirely clear whose side they were on. Their fire seemed to be directed primarily at the dinosaurs, but they weren't shy about blasting the occasional Monkeybots. Of course, they were only humans, after all. Terrible aim. Limited ability to coordinate complex tactical maneuvers. Highly unpredictable. If it weren't for that Treaty, TG-XLR7 would mow them down with his laser pen and simplify the battlefield a bit.

But, so long as the Key was lost in the human epoch, the Treaty was a necessary inconvenience.

The Key.

The background subroutines scrutinizing Larry registered a critical data point. New protocols overrode the Servodroid's primary programming. This was more like it. This was what TG-XLR7 was really here for.

Larry had the Key.

TG-XLR7 was going home!

NEXT THING I KNOW, that big butler robot grabbed at my arm. He lifted me up in the air trying wrench that Key thing from my grasp. There was no other choice but to make a counter-grab. I was pretty sure he would rip my arm of if I didn't.

When my other hand connected with the Key is when a whole new layer of trippy shit started happening.

The entire blue hazed landscape was suddenly very clear to me. There were actually features to it. Hills and things. Walls and obstacles. It wasn't really a boring, flat plane after all. And I could see everyone in it. Ishmael, Liz, a crap-ton of monkey robot ninjas fighting a butt-load velociraptors. And there were others, too. The Orb and Hastings and Lovejoy, of course, but there were also a couple dozen other blue jumpsuited time agents popping out of trenches and out from behind invisible boulders, toasting dinosaurs left and right with special timecop guns.

And then there was Cooper, that crazy ass son of a bitch, and his pack of wild dogs tearing into just about everything that got in their path.

That was one level of it, because, on top of it all, I could see a different world. Maybe it was the same world, but it was there. It was like looking at a reflection on a TV screen when you're zoning out during the commercials. Normally you just filter that out as you're watching the show, but then, when you're not actively trying to keep track of what crap Kramer and Newman are getting into, you see the glare from the lamp, the shape of the sofa, your stupid roommate's stupider brother. This was like that, only I was seeing Wal.

It roughly matched up with the shapes in the blue landscape, but it was frozen, like everything there was on pause. There was another battle raging in that place, too. Robot monkey ninjas, dinosaurs, some big dinosaurs. That Horkachorge guy, and Waldo, with his ridiculous sweater, and a few other huge, nasty carnivores. It became clear that some of what I thought were big blue boulders were actually allosaurs in zoot suits in the reflection world. There were so many. It was like the Hoth battle in Empire Strikes Back, except with actual freaking dinosaurs instead of AT-ATs.

The people of Wal were kind of caught in the cross-fire between the monkey ninjas and the dinosaurs. They were basically screwed. Lots of people were frozen mid-stride, running for the hills. Cooper, like I said, somehow brought his herd of wild dogs into the Time Barrier. Grampie Queequeg was back in Wal, though, and that surprised me. Hannie and Grampie Queequeg were holed up in what looked like a Mad Max Winnebago with a couple rocket launchers on top of it. I wonder where he dug that up. I couldn't tell if it was mobile or not. I hoped it was.

A few of the people of Wal, Stokes and his thugs mostly, were making an effort at putting up a fight, a hopeless effort on their part. I'll admit, it was more than a little satisfying to see an allosaur's mandible about to chomp down on Stokes' head. That guy messed with my girl. I couldn't wait to tell her his fate.

But first the butler robot had his agenda, and he really didn't seem to care if I was still holding onto the Key or not.

He took the Key over to that weird, dwarf doorway by the info desk. There was a keyhole, of course. I don't know why I didn't see that coming. The robot butler inserted the key, I had to adjust my grip to keep from losing a couple fingers, because that guy was not messing around.

He twisted the Key, and the archway expanded larger and larger until I realized all of Robot Hell was opening up before us. The Butler robot stepped through the archway. And me, natural born genius that I am, I kept hanging on. Holy shit!

Chapter 29
A Slight Case of Chronoclavis

(*Ishmael*)

I don't often think back to the days before I was a time traveler. They were wasted days. To be honest, I wasn't in any better position in life than Larry was when I met him. Okay. I had a watered down English degree from a state university. I had that much, which really isn't much. It was a piece of paper that said my dreams were bigger and wilder than I could ever realize.

My dreams...

When I was a kid I loved cartoons with giant robots in them. *Tranzor Z*, *Robotech*, even that Godzilla movie with Jet Jaguar in it. More than anything I wanted to be a giant robot, or, more precisely, a giant robot pilot. Getting behind the wheel of a Voltron lion or a Veritech Battloid, and defending hapless humans from evil, giant, alien beasts was my dream. Not only would it be personally fulfilling, but if I wasn't one of the husky guys who always died honorably in combat, I would definitely get a super hot, and possibly half-alien, girlfriend.

But 1999 came and went, and no alien artifact dropped out of the sky to crash on some remote island, jumpstart advanced robotics technology, and unite the human race against the inevitable alien invasion. None of that happened.

So, I culled my collections of comic books and imported Japanese toys, and tried to become a grown up. I wasn't very good at it. Mostly I perfected the art of how to get drunk efficiently and alienate all your friends and relatives. There are some disappointments you never get over. Mine was that I was never going to be robot jock no matter how many cardboard models and mock-ups I built.

That one sacred disappointment came back to hit me in the nethers when that archway opened up large enough for the Cyberian hospitality droid to waltz through. On the other side, in the land of a future forbidden to humanity, I could see the feet and lower legs of a Cyberian Gonzo-Destructo Mech.

It was awesome.

Not the watered down version of awesome that everyone uses these days. No. It was the biblical, 'I cower in helplessness before the almighty power of my creator,' definition of awesome.

"I have to drive that..."

"Too bad," said the Orb, "they're self-actuating."

The Orb was in full berserker-time-mutant fury. His unitard was torn and tattered. Blood, some of it his, some of it not, was smeared across his body. His head was a ball of lightning, with bursts of energy shooting out at seeming random, but always connecting with a velociraptor or two.

I'd never seen this side of the Orb. It was the truly terrifying side I never wanted to see, but always suspected was there.

He grabbed me by the elbow and pulled me to follow.

"This is all your grandfather's fault," he muttered.

"No argument here," I said. "But I'm not leaving Liz alone in the middle of this shitstorm."

"Fine," he said. "Bring your cousin."

"Cousin?" said Lizzabits.

"Also your grandfather's fault. Come on!"

The Orb took us in pursuit of the Servodroid and Larry, toward the archway that was now large enough for us to pass.

As we pushed toward it, we were shoved from behind by a crushing wave of little dinosaurs. The monkey ninja robots fell on the wave, dropping out of the skies, from out of nowhere, and through archway from the future. All the while blasts of lightning sheared off from the Orb's aura and toasted saurians and Cyberians alike.

Through the force of the Orb's will alone we found ourselves on the front doorstep of the robot empire that shall inherit the earth.

ADVANCED HOSPITALITY Servodroid TG-XLR7 was simultaneously elated and annoyed. Finally returning to its native timeframe after so many countless power cycles on concierge duty sent the servodroid into the deepest throes of simulated ecstasy that its programming allowed. It was that little snot of a human being clinging to TG-XLR7's arm that was diluting the mood.

Never mind that. TG-XLR7 wasn't going to let Larry, the horrible time traveler, spoil its homecoming.

AS SOON AS WE WERE through the archway, past the Great Time Barrier, an army of all sorts of robots, from the monkey ninja Observer model to the colossal Gonzo-Destructo Mechs and several types in between, closed ranks on us and trained their weapons.

"I need to interface with the Grand Adjuticatron," said the Orb.

An Advanced Hospitality Servodroid, designation JK-FTV4, stepped into the space between us and the quickly closing perimeter of cybernetic death machines.

"Request denied," it said. "You are in violation of the Epoch Territorial Establishment Treaty. Prepare to be incinerated."

"Turnabout is fair play," said the Orb. "You've been polishing your chassis posteriors with the Treaty all day.

"Prepare," the Servodroid said, "to be incinerated."

"I think not," said the Orb.

I always knew the Orb was powerful. I'd never really understood to what extent before. He didn't even flinch as the encircling soldierbots powered their weapons.

Liz grasped at my hand, and I grasped back.

"Does he know what he's doing?" she asked.

"I'm so far out my depth," I said. I kept clicking all the toggles on my watch, even the ones that I don't know what they do, but nothing happened. Even the music player function was dead.

"At least it's nice to be with family," she said. "I mean, if we have to die, at least we're not alone."

"Yeah," I said.

"Article 3," said the Orb, "section 7, subparagraph B of the Treaty clearly states that, in the event of immanent breach of the Time Barrier by entities from a non-signatory epoch, I get to come here and talk to the Grand Adjuticatron to coordinate a response."

"One moment," said the Servodroid. "Oh, yes. I see the relevant subparagraph. Yes. Well, the dinosaurs are indeed at the gates. But we've got this."

The Servodroid stepped backwards, and joined the wall of robots that were charging their weapons.

"Incinerate!"

Our circular firing squad unleashed a coordinated burst of firepower of science fictional proportions. We really should have been fried. But, like I said, I had no idea how truly powerful the Orb actually was.

Right when the robots' energy pulse should have fried us like so many over-microwaved burritos, a wreath of eldritch fire formed around us. The wreath extended up and down, meeting with itself, forming a protective dome over us. It was fed by an uncanny umbilical conduit of energy flowing straight from the middle of the Orb's forehead.

"Ishmael," the Orb groaned, straining to keep his timehead doing whatever it was his timehead was doing that kept us from being turned to ash. "Cover your eyes... Don't... don't look back... You're... you're going to have... to finish this... you have to finish this..."

And then, with a scream, the Orb's dome exploded outward.

In spite of his warning, I was still seeing spots. The wreckage was unbelievable. Every robot within a quarter mile, including the Gonzo-Destructo Mechs, were ripped apart and thrown across the landscape as though they'd been made of tin foil.

It was hard to make sense of it, to figure out which direction was forward.

"Oh gods," said Lizzabits. "I think I figured out which direction is 'back.'"

The Great Time Barrier was collapsing behind us, revealing another army, an army of dinosaurs who were taking advantage of the breach with all deliberate speed.

From the opposite direction I heard a groan.

"Larry!"

Liz rushed to him. I really don't get how those two made such a connection so fast. One of the benefits of being young and stupid, I suppose. It's easy to pair off.

"Someone get this effing robot off me," he said.

He was pinned to the ground by the still body of TG-XLR7.

We didn't have much time. The larger dinosaurs were covering ground quickly and deliberately.

Liz and I gave the robot hulk a shove, and it came to life again. Larry skittered out from underneath before it could make another grab for him.

"Stop," TG-XLR7 bleated. "The Key... the Chronoclavis..."

I didn't have time for any interference the severely damaged Servodroid might send us. Luckily there were a couple loose energy rifles nearby. I hefted one and hoped the old point and click method would be good enough.

It was.

I'd blasted a hole in its chest wide enough to leave the robot's head dangling by a few wires.

Larry grabbed the head and yanked it loose. He cut a strange image in that blast crater full of broken robots and scavenging dinosaurs. In one hand he had the Servodroid's cybernetic skull, in the other, the Key, *Chronoclavis* the droid called it, still clutched in the mummified fingers of whoever that poor son of a bitch was who lost his arm. Larry had come a long way since I'd met him. Perhaps there was something for Liz to see in him after all.

"This guy's been telling me stuff," said Larry. "This key ignites a weapon. A giant Time Bomb. The monkey ninjas have been looking for this thing for a long time. It got lost in some big time war you never told me about. Where that giant head dude, the Orb, and the robots were fighting over just who was allowed to screw with whose timeline. Apparently the robots have figured out several scenarios where they can tweak history just a little bit and they can get a jumpstart on their action. Like, they figured they'd have a more efficient time of setting up their empire with at least some petroleum at their disposal."

"I never knew about a time war," I said. "I always figured the CTCAHQ was just a clubhouse for jerks. It never occurred to me they were actually serving a purpose."

"Whatever," said Larry. "We've got to put some lead on it before those dinosaurs get what they're looking for."

Looking back, I could see more and more carnivorous thunderlizards popping into the landscape. With the Time Barrier out of commission, there was nothing to stop them from coming for what they wanted. And, if the robots wanted to find away to cut the human epoch short, the dinosaurs were most certainly looking for a way to extend their own.

More robots joined the battle, but it was clear that the Orb's dying act had seriously compromised the Cyberians defenses. There were no other Gonzo-Destructo Mechs in the immediate theater, and the smaller robots proved ineffective against wave after wave of fleet-footed carnivorous bipeds the size of school busses.

The dinos stampeded through the scorched crater, making a rush for territory deep behind Cyberian lines. We scrambled for cover behind the twisted body of one of the giant mechs that I wanted to pilot so badly. As we took position, the rushing dinosaurs passed by one after another, ignoring us completely.

The head of TG-XLR7 sparked to life in Larry's hand.

"You must get to the Field Generator, Larry," it said. "You're our only hope."

"What kind of cornball crap is that?" I said.

"If the dinosaurs get the Field Generator, they will take it back with them and prevent their mass extinction event. If you get there first, you can use the *Chronoclavis*," said the severed robot head.

"I thought the Key sets off the Time Bomb," said Larry.

"Among other things."

"What other things," I asked.

"Things," the robot said. "Things with time. Things with space."

"The robots wanted to set their Time Bomb off in 1989," said Larry. "Cut humanity out of the picture there, because they figured out how to start their whole civilization from a single Nintendo cartridge, or something."

"Something like that," said the robot head.

"But the way I figure it," said Larry, "is I'm from 1993. There's no way that bomb can go off in '89 if I'm the guy pulling the trigger. It's gotta violate some sort of time laws or something."

"Yes," said the robot. "Something like that."

"I don't trust these guys," I said. "I sure as hell don't trust the dinosaurs. And I never trusted the Orb, for that matter. The only thing

I know for sure is I don't want to see any of them get a hold of this Time Bomb. Let's go for it."

We climbed up a little higher on the mech's chassis to get a look at our destination.

"There it is," said the robot head. "Fifteen kilometers to the northeast. In the Citadel."

Of course there's a Citadel. A big robot citadel made of metal, concrete, pipes, gears and circuits. It looked like an inside-out plumbing department from a home improvement store. And between it and us was a battlefield full of legions of robot soldiers engaged in combat with rampaging hordes of allosaurs and t. rexes.

"Screw this," said Larry. "If we're going to get there, we're going to need a ride."

Chapter 30
Rock 'em Sock 'em

(*Larry*)

The thing is, while I'm admittedly not the most aware and enlightened guy, I was beginning to notice something about Ishmael. Basically, he wasn't even paying attention to Liz at all. Like she might not even have been there as far as he was concerned. I know I'm a little biased, because we were having some major chemistry in the middle of that epic dinosaurs vs. robot war going on all around us. I suppose it's only natural. But Ishmael could obviously give a crap.

Which is why I was absolutely struggling to hold it in while, as Ishmael and Robot Head and I were discussing our next moves, Liz was doing a status check on the giant piece of supersweet machinery we were hiding behind. She might be from some screwed up barbarian apocalypse time, but she's got a lot going on. Aside from being one hell of a kisser.

Yeah, I was still pretty charged up on that.

But back to business. As we were all worried about how the hell were going to move 15 clicks through all sorts of robot hell and get to that Citadel, Liz was figuring out some pretty interesting things about the Gonzo-Destructo Mech.

First of all, it's not a self-actuated robot in its own right. It's a giant robot that's driven by a smaller, person-sized robot. And it turned out that the driver robot was what was taken out when the Orb's head exploded. I guess his super weird mind bolts shot straight at the thinking circuits, or something? And the mech itself wasn't the thinker, the driver robot was.

I have no idea why the Cyberian Imperium thought it was a good idea to design their equipment like that, but it was fantastically convenient for us. Fantastically, unbelievably convenient.

Just as I was looking at the total shitstorm of robot on dinosaur violence we were going to have to wade through thinking, dammit, I wish we had a ride, Liz was like, "I think that can be arranged."

She had the Gonzo-Destructo Mech powered up and on its feet before I could even finish complaining about how impossible getting to the Field Generator in the Citadel was going to be.

It was a little awkward, because Ishmael and I were standing *on* the giant robot as Liz started moving it around. I had my hands full, with my severed, regular-sized robot head and my creepy severed hand with the Key that was either going to fix everything, or erase several hundred years of human history. I kind of slid down the side of the Mech's arm just as Liz brought it up to standing.

Ishmael, on the other hand, was pretty pissed. He climbed all the way up to the shoulder and tried to peel open the hatch to get inside.

"You don't understand!" he was shouting. "This is my thing! This is what I've always been meant to do!"

It was hilarious.

There was no way he was going to get that cockpit hatch open. It was sealed for battle, and Liz wasn't messing around.

While Ishmael was on the one shoulder, the giant Mech's hand grabbed me and put me on the other shoulder. Liz was a natural. Not only was Ishmael able to maintain his perch during that whole maneuver, I was not squished into silly putty. I was a little worried about that, but just for a minute. It was just so awesome to be able to ride on the shoulder of a Mech like that. (I may have played Battletech once or twice in junior high. Don't judge.)

So, as Ishmael was keeping his bitchfest going about how he was the oldest, he should be driving, Liz just put that puppy in gear.

I bobbed up and down with each step of the machine. Liz kept it going in a steady rhythm, pounding the earth with each footstep, but not so savagely that we'd be shaken off. It rocked. There's no other word for it. I couldn't help but hum that Black Sabbath song Beavis and Butthead love as we cut through the battle raging around us. *"Duh-duh, duh-duh-duh. Duddha-duddha-duddha duh duh duh!"*

I'm not sure if I expressed the size of the robot we were riding clearly. It's hard to judge, because I don't really think of things in terms of feet or meters. Let's just say the Gonzo-Destructo Mech was easily twice as tall as the T-Rexes that were running around.

A few of the T-Rexes made the mistake of attacking us. Liz just put a palm forward and shot a jet of super robot fire at them. It was like she was flash frying a giant chicken. And when she wasn't frying them, she was just stepping on them like she absolutely didn't give a shit. Which maybe she didn't.

We were making good time, and the robot armies all gave us plenty of room. Either they thought we were on their side, or they had a good knowledge of the Mech's specifications and just kept the hell out of the way.

"Liz, you are so hot right now," I said.

"I could be even hotter," she said. "Only you're sitting on the missile launcher exhaust ports and I'd rather not melt you. But don't test me."

"Yes, ma'am."

We were making excellent time.

While Ishmael kept whining about Tranzor Z and whatever over on the other shoulder, I was pumping the robot butler's head for information. He was actually pretty forthcoming. He seemed more afraid of the dinosaurs "precluding humanity and thence Cyberia" than anything I could possibly do to him. He told me exactly what I needed to know. I still didn't trust it, but I didn't have anything better to go with. It was the Hail Mary of Hail Marys. It would either work, or we'd be dead.

It was then that I realized just how much I'd grown since crapping my pants in that sewer earlier on. Basically, I noticed that I wasn't crapping my pants at that moment, and we were way more screwed.

Liz kept kicking dinosaur ass all the way to the walls of the Citadel. As we got closer it looked like there might be a couple obstacles in the way of getting me to Field Generator. And, by obstacles, I mean two more Gonzo-Destructo Mechs.

"Sorry guys," said Liz. "I'm going to need those missile launchers. Slide down the arms to the elbows."

"Your shitting me," I said. "I've got my hands full."

"Let me go, Larry," said the robot head. "There's no more I can tell you."

"But... but, I always wanted a robot head."

"Don't be stupid," said Ishmael as he shimmied down the giant left arm.

A panel opened up where he had been sitting revealing rack after rack of mini-missiles ready for Liz to pull the trigger.

"Effin' A," I said. "All right robot. You've been pretty decent to me, but I've got to see those puppies in action."

I chucked the robot head out into the battle below. I hoped he'd land on something relatively soft, but who was I kidding. It was bittersweet. He had tried to tear my arm out of its socket to get at the Key. But, he'd also been pretty cool about being reduced to just a head.

I slipped the Key into my waistband and scooted down the arm near me. There were lots of cables and wires and things to hold on to as I made my way.

"I'm going to jump," said Liz.

"What?"

"There's a map in here," she said. "The Citadel really isn't that big. A simple walled fort with the Field Generator right in the middle of it. Hold on."

The Mech picked up speed as we rushed to the wall. At the last moment, it jumped. As it was in midair, Liz sent a shower of shoulder missiles at each of the two other Mechs. It goes without saying that the jig was up. If the robots hadn't figured out our Mech was a rogue agent before, they knew for sure now.

When Liz hit the ground, we weren't all that far from the Field Generator. The Citadel was a clean, modern, robot death-fort without much clutter, so we had a clear shot. Unfortunately the impact of landing that super robo-jump had shaken both me and Ishmael loose from our perches. We spilled our asses all over the deck as Liz brought the Gonzo-Destructo Mech up into ready position.

The other two Mechs were shaking the dust off and turning to see just what the flip was going on. They were pretty dented up from the missile barrage, but still operational.

"We don't have a lot of time," said Ishmael. "You know what to do?"

"Dude," I said, "I never waste time *knowing* what to do. I just do it."

Ahead of us, pretty much in the dead center of the fort, was a giant knobby metal pyramid thing with a faint blue glow dripping out of the vents and cracks and stuff. It was pretty obvious that's where the Field Generator had to be, so we started hauling off for it. I pulled the Key thing out of my pants. The hand attached to it had lost a couple fingers in the impact. I sincerely hoped they weren't rolling around in my chonies, but who had time to check?

Ishmael lay down some covering fire with the blaster rifle he'd picked up earlier. But, honestly, there really weren't any robots around, aside from the two Mechs Liz was going hand to hand with.

I wish I could have watched that more closely than just the few stray glimpses I caught over my shoulder. She was wailing on them with an ass-kicking of such creative fury and ingenuity, I just wanted to get to know her better so I'd know how to stay on her good side. The woman was a force of nature, a hurricane unto herself, a Nirvana song embodied in human form driving a giant robot and beating the ever-living crud out of other giant robots. I had never witnessed anything so beautiful. If only I could have sat and watched, but there was shit needed to get done.

Ishmael and I made it to the base of the pyramid, but we were at a bit of a loss. It might not have been a full-size pyramid, but even a 1/16 scale pyramid was a lot to take in at once.

"I guess we look for a door or a keyhole or something?"

"And we'd better find it pretty quick," said Ishmael. "Look."

Liz had slammed one of the other Mechs into the Citadel wall so hard the wall split. There was a huge V of torn and bent metal, split from the top to about three quarters down. It was big enough for the dinosaurs to start spilling through.

"Damn," I said. "Remember that universal key fob remote thingy?"

"Yeah."

"Pretty awesome if we had that right now."

"Yeah?" said Ishmael, kind of hopeful, like he was wondering if I had it in my pocket or something.

"But we don't."

"Shut up and keep looking," he said. "Just shut up. And keep looking."

Chapter 31
Time Bomb!

(*Ishmael*)

It should have been me out there. It should have been me. I've given up on a lot of dreams in my life; I've shouldered a lot of disappointments. But this one...

The hell with it. Liz was a damned fine mecha pilot. It was no accident, either, I found out later. One of the gifts my progenitor had secretly given the Storemasters of Wal was a deluxe arcade video game with controls almost identical to those of the Gonzo-Destructo Mech. All those years that her paranoid father had kept her sequestered from the ebb and flow of humanity, Liz kept busy by playing that video game. She'd been training for this her whole life, she just didn't know it.

The only question was, did Gramps know what he was doing when he gave the game to the Storemasters? Who knows. He's a cagey bastard at best.

Liz was more than holding her own. She'd already evened the odds by taking out one of the two Mechs that were on palace guard duty in the Citadel. Of course, things can't stay the same for too long.

Through the smoking hole Liz had put in the Citadel wall, a flow of dinosaurs had begun to burst forth.

Immediately, Liz and the other Gonzo-Destructo Mech set their differences aside and focused their aggression on the common enemy. Even though the Mechs dwarfed the dinosaurs, they were ridiculously outnumbered. It was as if the entire Mesozoic Era was spilling through the breach. Maybe it was. It's conceivable that their extinction event was the stressor that triggered their time travel method. Or maybe it was their special taco meat. Who knows? Whatever the reason, whatever the cause, there were a hell of a lot of them and they were coming on fast.

Liz and the other Mech did their best to staunch the flow, but there were just too many.

Meanwhile, Larry and I were scrambling all over the face of the central pyramid looking for anything that the Key might fit into.

"We're screwed," said Larry. "We're screwed, we're screwed, we're screwed!"

"Less talky, more lookie!" I said.

The lightweight velociraptors were the first to slip past both Mechs. They were stampeding for the pyramid. When they got within 80 yards, the pyramid itself came to life. Scores of small laser turrets emerged from the pyramid walls and started blasting the creepy, feathered sons of bitches.

It was clear the velociraptors scored a higher threat rating than Larry or I did. There's no way we could have just slipped past security. I was almost insulted that we hadn't been skewered by lasers as well.

"Oh, come on!" I shouted. "I know you know we're out here!"

"FINE," said an electronic voice that reverberated through the entire Citadel. "COME INSIDE."

A panel of the pyramid's metal sheathing slid open in front of us. The electronic voice didn't have to invite us twice.

WE WERE IN A NO-FRILLS corridor lined with conduits, blinking lights, and low head room. It was more of a maintenance tunnel than a proper hallway. We didn't spend much time worrying about whether to proceed deeper into the pyramid because we could already hear the dinosaurs pounding on the panel that had already closed behind us.

"Hello?" I called.

There was no answer.

"I think that voice was the Grand Adjudicatron," said Larry.

"How would you know?"

"My robot head told me a lot of stuff before I had to chuck him. One of the things he said was about the badass Grand Adjuticatron voice that's pretty much the leader of the robot guys. And that we shouldn't bother trying to kiss his ass, because he hates that crap."

"Shouldn't be a problem," I said. "Do you know where we're going?"

"Away from the dinosaurs, dude."

Fair enough. We made our way further down the tunnel, ducking our heads and searching in the faint, blinking light for anything resembling a keyhole.

"WHAT'S TAKING YOU SO LONG?" asked the voice.

"Well," said Larry, "It's kind of dark in here."

"I DON'T SEE HOW THAT'S MY PROBLEM."

My head hit a low hanging cross-brace. I had to curse quite a bit.

"Well, it's a problem for us," said Larry. "We're simple, flawed humans who have trouble getting around in the dark."

"ARE YOU ATTEMPTING TO VERBALLY PROSTRATE YOURSELF?"

"This has nothing to do with my prostate," said Larry. "What the hell's wrong with you?"

"LET ME CHOOSE PLAINER TERMS. ARE YOU TRYING TO KISS MY ASS?"

"You can kiss *my* ass," I said. "Your whole civilization is going down the shitter if the dinosaurs get in here and get their talons on the Field Generator."

"REALLY? HOW DO YOU FIGURE?"

"Well, they're going to use it to deflect their asteroid, or whatever it is they need to do to prevent the Cretaceous-Paleogene extinction event."

"YOU DON'T KNOW THAT."

"No," I said, "but why else would they be here?"

"*THE CODEX AND CATALOGUE OF ORGANIC HISTORICAL MOTIVATIONS* IS INCONCLUSIVE ON THIS TOPIC, BUT I THINK IT MAY BE THAT THEY'VE HEARD ABOUT OUR RESTAURANTS."

"Bullshit!" I said. "Look. Those hordes of dinosaurs? They're not exactly foodies. If you ask me, they found out a giant asteroid was going to destroy their way of life and they decided to do something about it."

"YOU'RE REALLY GRASPING AT STRAWS, NOW."

"You've got the technology."

"WE ARE TECHNOLOGY."

"And there would be no technology without humans."

"LOOK WHO'S FEELING SELF-IMPORTANT NOW?"

"Self-important!"

"He's just stalling us," said Larry. "You know that, right?"

"What?"

"WHY WOULD I DO THAT? DISTRACTION, MISDIRECTION AND OBFUSCATION ARE HARDLY THE CYBERIAN ETHOS."

"Oh, I bet you're just keeping us talking to distract us while a crack team of monkey ninjas tracks us down and grabs the key."

"NOW THAT'S AN IDEA. QUITE A GOOD ONE, ACTUALLY. YOU KNOW, I ACTUALLY HAVE AN OPENING ON MY ADVANCED STRATEGIC CONCEPT AND PLANNING TEAM. YOU MIGHT BE AN IDEAL CANDIDATE FOR THE POSITION."

"Now you're kissing my ass," said Larry. "But it won't do you any good. I found what I'm looking for."

"What?"

"WHAT?"

"Yeah," said Larry. "I'm surprised, too, but I'm turning this key."

This kid was truly charmed by some strange force of cosmic justice I would never truly be able to understand. In the dark, in the heart of a cold, calculating robot empire that couldn't care less if we lived or died, Larry found the ultimate Easter egg, the main override switch on the Field Generator. It was behind a box marked 'hamdingers'.

"YOU REALLY SHOULDN'T—" the Grand Adjudicatron protested, but it was too late.

Larry turned the Key, switching it from Time Barrier mode to Time Bomb mode.

Everything exploded. It was a flash of time energy like I had never seen. Everything was silhouetted against everything else, and back again. Everyone was everywhere. It was like one of those movies from the 1960s where they were playing with interesting ways of deliberately processing the film wrong instead of inventing actual special effects. I wanted to vomit, but I couldn't figure out where my mouth was.

And then it was over. I was somewhere with no dinosaurs and no robots. It was somewhere familiar, with rolling, grassy hills and a nice shady tree nearby. The air was fresh and the sun was warm. It was nice to be alive. I was fairly sure Larry was alive somewhere, too. I wasn't certain, but I was fairly sure. I was also fairly sure there wasn't much I could do about anything. I'd been going on adrenaline for longer than I could keep track and suddenly I was in a quiet, warm afternoon with muscles that were no longer interested in holding my bones upright.

All things being equal, I took a nap.

Epilogue

(*Larry*)

After I set off the Time Bomb, all I wanted to do was barf. It was like the worst time jump ever. No tacos were involved, and I really wasn't sure if I might be dead. At some point I decided to just lie down and close my eyes. I have no idea how long it was before someone started kicking me.

"Well, Larry, you did it," the kicker was saying.

I cracked open my eyelids and immediately regretted it. There was Grampy Queequeg.

"What do you want?"

"I'm helping Ishmael round up everybody that got hit by the blast," he said.

"He asked you to do that?"

"No," he said. "As a rule, we don't talk to each other. It usually means one of us is about to die. But Cooper asked me to lend a hand in rounding everyone up and bringing them back to headquarters. Then, when I demurred, he started telling me many, many things I didn't want to know."

"Cooper? How is that weirdo?"

"Not good," said Gramps. "He was at the apex of the pyramid when you threw the switch. He was in the middle of everything. He says he saw the whole course of human history before it was done with him."

"He's the same dude as the Knowledge, isn't he?" I said.

"Who else would he be?"

"I knew it. I knew I knew him from somewhere." But I'm also pretty sure I ran into him at a Dead show. It's too bad Cooper's nowhere near coherent enough to get down his take of events. All I can do is surmise that, as soon as the Time Barrier was down, he and his pack of wild dogs went apeshit all over the future, fighting the velociraptors who were scouring the outside of the pyramid, looking for their own way in to grab the Field Generator. Makes sense, but who knows. All that's for certain is he was right at ground zero when the Time Bomb went off. I would say 'poor dude,' but having seen what he was like before, and after, I really can't judge whether or not the whole thing might have actually been good for him. Also, I saw how he dies.

Thinking of that was really heavy. I didn't like that.

"Come on, space cadet," said Gramps. "There's somebody waiting for you."

"If it's all the same, I'm kind of really ready for a break from Ishmael."

"Not Ishmael," said Gramps. "Lizzabits."

I was up on my feet. He didn't have to tell me twice.

THE ROBOT HEAD, TG-XLR7, had explained it to me like this:

"The Time Bomb is the kindest kind of bomb, really. It doesn't kill anyone. It's just a more powerful version of the Time Barrier. Instead of keeping entities from passing a certain threshold in history, it just bounces them all back to the beginning of their own period."

I guess that's why we all found ourselves in Africa back in what Ishmael calls The Time of Chimpanzees. It was him and me, the usual jokers in the Cross Time Coordinating Agency Headquarters, and just about everybody from Wal that got caught up in that battle royal with the dinosaurs and robots.

With the Orb gone, the Cross-Time Agency guys all decided to vote Ishmael in as their new king, or supreme leader, or captain. I'm not even sure what they call it. I just call him 'Hoss.' Ishmael was highly annoyed at the prospect of being the head timecop, but at the same time he wasn't about to let anyone else take the reins once he had them.

But I didn't really care about that. What I cared about was that, when I stumbled into HQ, as soon as she saw me Liz pulled me close and tight. No matter what else is going on, if you've got a gorgeous human being who wants to hold you like that, you've really got something.

Also, I was looking forward to being there for the creation of history's first taco. I was hungry something fierce.

Andrew Coltrin / Larry the Horrible Time Traveler /

About the Author

Although he will often deny this at parties, Andrew Coltrin's fiction is not actually based on his own experiences as a time traveler. That line never really gets him anywhere at parties anyway. At various points in his life, Coltrin has worked in bookstores, coffee shops, and special education classrooms. He tends to regard various modes of rail transportation as members of his extended family and owns more manual typewriters than is absolutely necessary. Once upon a time he made zines about being abducted by terribly mundane aliens who forced him to wear polyester and sell tickets at a movie theater. Now he's too busy checking Facebook on his smartphone to play with photocopiers. Which is a shame. I hope he's proud of himself and what he's done to his family.

About the Publisher

Partly Robot Industries is the pet project of Andrew Coltrin. The great Kurt Vonnegut, Jr. observed in his book *Breakfast of Champions* that all of us human beings are broken robots, but at they same time we are also all unwavering bands of light. Partly Robot is dedicated to finding that unwavering band of light. Also fun stuff. Look for more at www.partlyrobot.com